Locked Up or Covered Up

Locked Up or Covered Up, Volume 1

Dakota Wright

Published by Silver Maple Publishing, 2024.

This is a work of fiction. Similarities to real people, places, or events are entirely coincidental.

LOCKED UP OR COVERED UP

First edition. October 4, 2024.

ISBN: 979-8227094193

Written by Dakota Wright.

Table of Contents

I want to say thank you to all the people who have supported me in writing this book. It took alot of phone interviews, letters, and visits to the prison. And thank you to my new readers, I hope you enjoy!

Lol, if you are looking for an everyday type of story full of love and romance and happy endings, you won't get that here.

You're about to enter my world and I hope you enjoy it!

My goal is to publish realistic urban fiction.

Please leave reviews and feel free to reach out to me and share your experience of reading my novel.

Thank you and God Bless!

Chapter 1

Regrets 1980

"Derrick! Danny! Get in this house! This storm is kicking up!" Mama yelled from the porch. The clouds hung low and the wind was stirring up trash. Me and Danny was in the middle of the street throwing a football. Then the tornado sirens started blasting. We ran into the house. Mama yanking us into the living room and then in the basement until the storm passed over us. I wanted my dad there but he was out in the streets. I would sleep on the couch every night to wait for him to walk through the front door.

On that night, I fell asleep on the couch and I woke up to him and Mama whispering.

"Derrick, you robbed that liquor store, didn't you?"

"Woman I ain't depending on Welfare to feed my family!"

I kept my eyes shut and pretended to be in a deep sleep.

"I'm not taking that money!" I heard Mama crying.

"Berenise! I risked my life to take care of you and them boys!"

"You not taking care of us robbing!"

"I gotta go!" Daddy said

I jumped up. "Daddy don't leave us!"

He turned to me then to Mama, "I gotta lay low for a few days. Let things blow over."

Then he disappeared out the front door leaving me and Mama at a loss for words.

Red and blue lights flashing it seemed like every cop car was surrounding our house.

"Police open up!"

It was the Summer of 1980. We were home one evening chilling when we heard fists pounding on our door. The living room floor shook at every knock. I was twelve years old and Danny was nine. Mama and our Daddy Big Rick was sitting on the couch watching Miami Vice. Me and Danny was on the floor playing monopoly.

"Derrick Gates! We have a warrant for your arrest! Open up!"

Two more floor shaking knocks. Big Rick leaped off the couch and ran to the back door. When Big Rick opened it, three cops with loaded guns were standing there waiting to blast him. Red and blue lights flashing it seemed like every cop car was surrounding our house.

We didn't see Big Rick no more after that night. Momma got tired of me and Danny asking about him then one day she told us, "He died in prison!" She whispered and that was the end of that. I always wondered why she never shed a tear.

We ended up moving to the Cochran projects in downtown St. Louis. Mama was sad that she had to give up our apartment that had windows that ran from the ceiling to the floor. Me and Danny was happy to be living in the same building as our cousins. It was so much life in the Jets. Memories that I will carry in my heart forever.

The jets can be grimy but all our family was there. People from my dad's side and all of Mama's sisters lived at the Cochran.

Three years later some shit went down at Aunt Irene's pad. Aunt Irene is Mama's oldest sister. Man, she loved me and Danny like we were one of her kids and Aunt Irene had five boys, Quinton, the twins Casey and Corey, Jeffrey, and Lil Man Man and she had one girl we called her Candy Cane.

We were all posted up at Aunt Irene's pad. Marvin Gaye was blasting through the 4 ft speakers. It was three card games going down at the same time. Aunt Irene had a lady frying fish and making plates to sell to the card players. Some of the players bought they gals with them to watch them lose or leave with fat wads in they pockets.

Me and Danny was running around with our cousins.

Mama kept dancing with this dude that kept following her all night. Everybody called him Pepper. He wore his hair long. It was curly and it hung to his shoulders. The nigga reminded me of Phillip Michael Thomas from Miami Vice. I thought he was a pimp.

Three months later Mama told me and Danny that she was pregnant by Pepper. She had cooked us hot cakes that morning. I almost choked when she announced it would be another mouth to feed and the thought of Pepper moving in with us churned the food in my stomach. Six months later, my Lil brother Michael was born. Pepper came to check him out then he bounced. We never seen him again. It was just me, Danny, Michael, and Mama.

A fight broke out during a card game and one of the hustlers got flaming mad because he was losing all his chips so he pulled out his gun and pointed to the ceiling. Everybody flew out of Aunt Irene's apartment.

Aunt Irene's hustle was card parties. Rufus her boyfriend, was always posted at the front door collecting money. Rufus and his long barrel pistol greeted all the thugs and street women who was looking to earn some of the winnings from the card games. Auntie lost her Section eight and 'ne day when she got home from the meat market an eviction notice was posted on her door.

When Auntie moved, Mama decided to move too and Aunt Zelda, Mama's youngest sister. We all moved within one block of each other, to North St. Louis.

Two months after we moved to our new spot, Mama and Larry come walking through the front door.

I knew he was a clown ass nigga on sight. He was rolling a toothpick around in the left corner of his mouth, sucking on his teeth. Red flashed in my eyes. I didn't hear a thing; I only caught his name.

The next day he showed up with his clothes stuffed in two black garbage bags. He was wearing dingy white overalls and a faded white hat with black combat boots. The front of his boots and the soles was caked in mud.

Mama bragged that he was a construction worker.

Right away that fool was acting like he was the king of the castle!

I took to the streets to get away from the shit that was going down at home. The first time Larry beat on Mama was on a Friday night. Mama had been waiting on Larry to get home because Friday was his payday.

I was ear hustling while playing Spades with Danny. We were all chilling in the living room. Michael was on the floor playing with his trucks.

"Irene as soon as he gets here, I need you and Rufus to drive me downtown to Olive Street so I can pay Laclede Gas."

Danny was on a roll that night, he had a winning hand. I threw down my cards in defeat.

"Girl the deadline to pay is today or they gon shut my gas off. Larry said he coming straight home as soon as he cashes his check."

Larry didn't get home until later on that night.

We was all in bed. Danny slept on the top bunk and Michael was sleeping on the bottom bunk. I was awake laying in my twin bed. Sleep finally hit me then Mama's screams pierced through the walls of our bedroom. I jumped out the bed and raced to her.

Larry had Mama pinned up against the wall slapping her with his right hand and his left hand was balled up into a fist and planted on her chest.

I knocked Larry off of her by pushing him into one of the end tables.

"Get off my Mama!"

"Derrick go back to yo room!" Mama yelled.

Mama's shaky voice sent shock waves through my body. I never heard my Mama's voice filled with pain not even when my Daddy was taken away in handcuffs.

Larry was struggling trying to get his balance back. I didn't move my feet concrete. I ran up on him, clocking him with my fist, his nose turned into a blood fountain. Next thing I know, I'm flying in the air. He snatched me around my waist and flung me across the living room. My body crashed into wall and I fell hard onto the hardwood floor. Larry kicked me in my side and his massive fist pounded my eyes. One blow to my head and he put me to sleep. I was knocked out for a few minutes.

"Larry please...stop. Don't hurt my babies!"

I woke up to Larry was beating Danny with one of his thick leather belts. Danny was balled up like a baby next to the couch. Lil Michael was hiding under the kitchen table crying.

Larry stopped beating Danny and turned to Mama and started whipping her with the belt.

I sat up my head pounding and then I crawled towards Mama's screams. Holding onto the arm of the couch I stood up and ran up to Larry to get him off of Mama. He snatched my arm and twisted it behind my back. My shoulder bone felt like it was to pop out the socket.

He pushed me to the front door. When he yanked it open, he squeezed my arm extra tight like he wanted to snap my bones into sticks and threw me out on the porch and locked the door.

"Nooo!" Mama's screams reached out into the street. I kicked the door with my bare foot and punched it ignoring the pain stabbing the bones in my hands. I could hear furniture scraping the hardwood floors. The door wouldn't budge, I cried for my Mama and my brothers.

I ran barefoot fifteen minutes barefoot straight not stopping to breath even though my chest felt like it was about to explode onto the concrete sidewalk. The anger and fear pumped me with the fire I needed to get to Aunt Irene's house.

"Oh Lord! What happened Derrick?" Aunt Irene screamed as soon as she opened the door.

"Larry!" Was all I could say then I collapsed out of breath. My face feeling like it was the size of the Good Year blimp.

"Rufus!" She yelled her voice bouncing off the hallway walls.

"Damn who beat this boy like this?" Rufus asked.

"Get him to the couch!" Uncle Rufus picked me up like I was a bag of potatoes. The cushions from the couch took the edge off the pain.

"Here baby put this on your eye!" Auntie covered my right eye with a bag of frozen something.

Uncle Rufus rounded up my uncle Harold, and my uncle Michael, the one my little brother was named after.

They beat the brakes off Larry and kicked him out of our house. Aunt Irene kept me at her crib for a few days. When I returned home, Mama had few words for me and that sliced through my heart big time. "When I tell you to stay outta my business I mean it dammit!" Even though, that goon was gon, a dark cloud was floating through the house.

A month later, when me and Danny came home from school, Larry and Mama was sitting at the kitchen table laughing and talking. Mama moved him back into the house and that's when the streets became my home.

Chapter 2

Goddess
"Gigi"

Me and JD, was sitting on the benches plotting on which corner store we was gon rob. Cory, Casey's twin, was sitting on the bench next to me reading a car magazine. Cory was the quiet dude out of all of us. All he wanted to do was read about cars and try to fix up that 1970 tan Maverick, Aunt Irene had parked in her backyard. We hit up all the corner stores near our Middle School so we had to go outside the hood. "Aye it's a spot on Natural Bridge. An old man runs it. You can flip over the chip stands and I can snatch up what we need and sell some of that shit at school." JD said.

"That's what's up!" I told him.

Casey jogged over to us. "Yo Danny, Goddess crying man!"

I hopped up from the bench ready to knock somebody out about my girl. Goddess Fletcher, always turned me down but I put claims on her fine ass since the first day she walked into Ms. Davis's class and every lil nigga at Turner Middle School knew not to step to her.

Me, JD, Casey, and Cory jogged over to where Casey spotted her crying and she wasn't there. Tracy, one of the girls Goddess hung with was talking to Adrianna. I stepped to Tracy. "What happened to my girl?"

"None of yo business, Goddess don't like you!" Tracy was brown skinned with short hair. She was one of those ugly girls who didn't cry if you talked about her nappy hair or her ugly sweaters.

I started to tell her bald-headed ass off but JD stepped in.

"Hey Tracy when you gon let me walk you home?" JD put his game down.

"Jeffrey, I thought you was going with Kay Kay?" she rolled her neck.

JD hated when somebody called him by his government name.

"Kay Kay don't go to this school no more. I ain't seen that girl. What's up wit me and you?"

"Meet me by the gate after school." She smiled.

"What happened wit Goddess?" he got close up in her face like they was about to kiss.

"Jermaine put gum in her hair." She said then the bell rang for us to go back to class.

After school, me, Casey, and Cory followed Jermaine as he walked home. JD bounced with Tracy to walk her home. Two blocks away from the school, Jermaine spotted us following him and he stopped walking and let us catch up to him.

"Danny, can I roll with y'all?" Jermaine was a light skinned pretty boy. He had a Geri curl and wore it long like the girls. I hated niggas wit long hair. He was taller than me but that didn't mean shit.

I walked up to him and said, "Fuck naw!" then I punched him dead in his nose. Blood squirted out his nose like a fountain, spilling all over his pink button up shirt.

"Damn man, what you hit me for?" he was bent over.

"Shut up, weak ass nigga!" Casey said with his fist ready.

"I told all y'all niggas to stay away from my girl!" I told him.

"Who yo girl?" blood covering his hand.

"Goddess!" I said.

"And next time we gon beat yo ass like we yo Daddy!" Casey said.

Cory just stood by the side peeping the scene.

Jermaine tried to run but Casey punched him in the back of the head and he stumbled. A crowd of kids surrounded us. I pushed his ass to the ground and one of his homies, Stan stepped to me.

Cory got in between us. "You want some of this?" Cory asked him.

"Nah, man!" Stan said and helped Jermaine get up off the sidewalk.

"Let's go shopping!" Casey said then we headed to the new corner store on Natural Bridge Avenue.

"Damn man why you shoving food in yo mouth?" Casey asked me.

I ignored him stuffing the Red Hot Riplets chips in my mouth. The spices burning the insides of my mouth then I finished the ham sandwich. We robbed the store. I snatched up five sandwiches from the cooler. Casey turned over the chip stand and grabbed up ten bags of chips and Corey stole the candy. What I couldn't tell my cousins was, Larry sometimes wouldn't let me and Lil Michael step into the kitchen. Mama would be working until nine o'clock at night. After I finished my sandwich and chips I reached for the Now and Laters candy.

"D don't take all the candy fool!" Casey yelled.

"Chill, I'm getting some for Goddess." I told him.

"Man, you and this chic." Casey said. "Why she get some? She ain't put in work at that store!"

"Mind yo business Casey." I told his ass.

The next morning at school, we was in the cafeteria eating breakfast. I spotted Goddess sitting at one of the tables by herself. Her friends hadn't got to school yet so I stepped to her.

"Danny get away from me." Her long hair was in a long braid down the middle.

"Here I got these for you." I slid three packs of grape Now & Laters in front of her. They landed next to the Cocoa puffs cereal in the plastic bowl.

"How you know I like grape?" she smiled.

"I know a lot of shit about you girl. Like for one, you ain't gotta worry about that fool Jermaine fuckin wit you."

"I'm still not yo girl." She turned her head away from me but I could see a smirk on her lips.

"Whatever! These other fools know they better not step to you cause they know you my girl Gigi."

She snapped her head back towards me frowning and smiling, we face to face. "What you call me?"
"Gigi!"
She smiled big then I knew she was mines.

Chapter 3

Alex Holmes a.k.a "Nine"

"Y'all niggas is slippin!" I barked at Blackboy and Rasheed. They was five minutes late for the drop.

"Nine man..." Blackboy started with his bullshit excuses.

I raised my hand and said, "Fuck the small talk. We got two hours to get this shit unpacked and take it to the cave!" The cave was the basement of the bakery I owned.

I arrived two hours before the drop.

I got to the restaurant before Blackboy and Rasheed. Vito, my supplier was never late. He delivered product on the 30th of every month. We hauled all the boxes to the basement.

"Let's do this!" I ordered Blackboy and Rasheed. I opened my safe and stashed half of the cocaine inside. Blackboy and Rasheed got dressed in aprons and masks. They dumped the white powder into a gigantic mixing bowl.

"Y'all down there?" Chef Mac my chemist had arrived on time.

"Yeah, Chef we getting it ready!" I yelled. Chef Mac was my chemist. He cooked up the cane after we unpacked the bricks. He stood at 5'11 and weighed 300 pounds. Mac used to play college football until he busted his knee.

Chapter 4

Regrets

One day me and my homie Ace was leaving the boxing gym. Ace was practicing his moves in the ring so he could have get a shot at winning a title belt. He was posted up at that spot 24/7. The gym was downtown on Washington Avenue. Ace wanted to go check out his Pops. His Pops lived on Cass and Grand Ave.

We walked and chopped it up. His Pops didn't answer his door. Pops lived in a two-family flat on the second floor.

"Let's grab some food while we wait on yo Pops."

We walked to London and Sons, a chicken joint ten blocks away.

"You got me? Cause you know I'm broke!" I told him.

"Man you know I ain't got no fights lined up. I ain't got it either!"

"Damn that chicken smell good!"

I said mad that I couldn't get shit.

"Let's go back to my Pop's pad I know he got some food. He should be home by now!"

"We gon get the money we need standing right here!" I told him.

"I ain't robbing nobody!"

"Shut you scary ass up and learn!" I schooled him.

A lady pulled up got out her car and just as she was reaching for the door handle, I reached for the door and opened it for her. "Excuse me Ms.? Do you have any spare change?"

She reached into the front pocket of her jeans and pulled out two crumbled up bills and shoved them into my hand then disappeared inside the restaurant the smell of fried chicken floating outside the restaurant, hitting my nose.

"Man all we got is two dollars!"

"Quit bitching up. You got the next person that pull up!" I said.

A apple red two door BMW with gold rims sped into the lot and parked close to the door. Two dudes was rolling in that car. Everybody on the lot was digging the ride. When the driver stepped out, I spotted a black bulge sticking out of his waist. It was the handle of a gun.

When he noticed me checking out his gun, he pulled down his Polo shirt to hide it.

"Nine! What up!" Ace walked up to the dude and they slapped each other five.

"You still hitting those punching bags?" Polo shirt asked Ace. This dude was sporting a gold watch and starched blue jeans and gold rimmed sunglasses. The other dude wit him had on all black. Black tee shirt, black jeans, and white Nikes with the black Swoosh sign.

"I'm still in the game Cuzzo!" Ace told him.

"Aye Black boy" Nine turned to the dude that was riding in the passenger seat. " This dude right here gon be the next heavyweight!" They all laughed.

"This my homie Derrick!" Ace pointed to me.

"What up!" Nine spoke.

I slapped him five.

"Come on let me hook ya'll lil niggas up!" Nine said.

We followed him and Black boy inside.

"Get what y'all want!" Nine asked. Me and Ace ordered the ten-piece chicken meal.

Then Nine ordered. "Gimme a hundred 100 wings, ten fries, and throw in some extra bread my man!" He told the man taking at the front counter.

"Damn who you feeding?" Ace asked him.

"My crew!" Nine said. He reached into his left front pocket and pulled out a fat wad of bills. He peeled off two-hundred-dollar bills and handed it to the man taking his orders.

I couldn't wait to drill Ace about this dude.

While we waited on them to cook our food, we posted up outside. The first thing Nine said to us was, "I can put some money in y'all pockets instead of the change y'all standing out here begging for!"

Ace's eyes got big. I gave him a blank stare cause I couldn't let him know that I was fucked up about what he knew what we was doing.

"How you know Cuzzo?"

"I got eyes everywhere!"

Me and Ace walked back to his Pop's crib. We sat on the steps and ate our food.

"We need to Holla at my cousin." Ace said as he bit into his wing.

"You ain't tell me you had a cousin that was a hustler." I said as I ripped my sauce covered wing in half with my teeth.

"He my first cousin my Auntie's oldest son."

"What's up with him? Ya'll ain't too tight you never mentioned that nigga to me!" I told him.

"Nine older than us. He hood rich."

"You gon wait on this boxing shit to kick off or go work for him?"

" I need bread in my pocket now. My girl pregnant."

"Damn Ace, for real?"

"Yeah man. Something gotta kick off you feel me?"

"A wright since you gon be a Daddy...

"Tomorrow we gon roll up to his spot and see what he rapping about!"

" I ain't going to no dope set!" I told him.

"Nigga he got a restaurant on Jefferson."

"Why he pull up to London and Sons then?"

"It's an after-hours joint but he there during the day you know making moves having hood meetings and shit."

"Bet! This hood rich nigga better be talking about putting some real bread in our pockets." I told Ace.

"He legit!"

Chapter 5

The Feds is Watching
Alex "Nine" Holmes

I spotted this cat sitting in the back of the bakery nursing a cup of coffee. He sat at that same spot for 3 hours. Every time, I turned his way, I caught him mugging me. His face looked familiar too but I couldn't place him. Every morning, at 6:00 am I pull up at the bakery I own. I sit, have a cup of coffee, call my Mama, then I read the newspaper. Bought it for cheap in 1984 because the owners was going bankrupt and wanted to shut it down. I hired a cat, to fix the paper work so I was legit. The fella dressed in the crisp suit gave me a nervous stomach.

"Boss you want another cup?" one of my employees walked up.

"Nah I'm good for now. Those croissants out the oven?"

"Yep, I'll bring you one!" she smiled and disappeared in the back.

Dude put his hat on, stood up, and walked out the bakery without making eye contact with me. My nerves kicked up and my senses went into defense mode because something told me that he was the Feds.

Chapter 6

Regrets

The next day in the afternoon me and Ace met up at Tucker Ave. We walked to Nine's restaurant, **The Flame**. The restaurant was in the middle of an incense shop and a cigar store on the South Side on Jefferson Ave.

One of his goons was posted at the door and a "We closed" sign handwritten in black marker was taped on the glass door. When the goon spotted me and Ace, he stood behind the door stoned faced. Dude was wearing a red and white t-shirt and red shorts.

"Nine here?" Ace shouted thru the door.

"Maybe? Who wanna know?" The dude had too many teeth in his mouth.

" Ace. "

"This some bullshit!" I said.

"Yo chill!" Ace said then too many teeth came back and I could hear the deadbolt locks clicking open.

When we stepped inside the smelled of bleach hit my nostrils and I wanted to gag so I held my breath. Teeth led us to a booth in the back of the restaurant. I could barely see except for the slice of light coming from the kitchen. Male voices was talking over the sound of metal pots and pans clanking together.

"Hey!" I whispered to Ace. " They don't believe in turning on the lights up in this mug?"

Ace threw up his hands.

I was ready to jet but then Nine and two of his goons appeared. He led the way to the booth and they stayed in the background.

He had a white plastic apron on and he was wearing white gloves.

"Got a job if y'all ready to start!" Nine spoke up.

"We ready to get it!" Ace fired back.

I mean mugged Ace. "Depends on what we doing?" I jumped in.

"I'ma lay it all out for you niggas. You know Porter?"

"Yeah he hustle on the West side!" Ace opened up his big mouth.

"He the first assignment!" Nine said his voice flat and cold.

"You want us to take him out?" Ace asked.

"Nah just give em a warning!" Nine said then one of his goons stepped up.

and whispered something and handed him a cordless phone. Nine slid out the booth and stood up covering up the phone.

"Ace make sure you home later."

"Why?"

"Special delivery!" He didn't wait for us to ask any questions he walked away and disappeared in the back of the restaurant. That fool just knew we wasn't gon turn down the job.

On the way back to the Cochran projects we stopped and grabbed a box of chicken fried rice. We was so broke we had to share it.

Ace didn't leave his apartment. I stayed to see what the special delivery was gon be.

At 5 o'clock that evening it was a knock on the door. I yelled to the door "Who is it?"

"Got yo food order!" A dude's voice answered from the other side.

Ace got up while I stood behind the door holding a bat.

Ace got the bag from him then the dude told him, "Here yo car keys!"

"I ain't got no car!"

The dude dropped the keys on the floor and bounced.

Ace snatched up the keys and slammed the door.

I reached for the bag it was a white oversized paper bag, the cardboard bucket that chicken wings come in was stuffed inside the bag. I lifted it out the bag and the box was heavy. My heart started pounding.

"Open it!" Ace sounded nervous.

I peeled back the top and two handguns was inside.

Holding the steel in my hand made the job real.

Ace's house phone rung.

"Our ride is set. Let's go!" Ace said after he hung up the phone.

It was eighty- five degrees that night and the air was humid. The heat was rising from the asphalt making the air hard to breathe. When I heard a car door slam I jumped.

"Calm the fuck down!" Ace whispered.

We hid in a gangway next to this bar called the Rose. It was a poppin bar on Natural Bridge Avenue where the old heads used to party. Natural Bridge was a busy street up until midnight. The best part about it was most of the block had the street lamps blown out.

A line of people was waiting outside the club to be let in. My gut was nervous because I didn't want us to be spotted. Food cooking from a nearby chicken joint made my stomach growl. All of a sudden, I didn't want to be down with this job. Brakes squealing from a car rolling down Natural Bridge made my heart jump.

Then a bum walked across the gangway pushing a shopping cart. It took every nerve in my body not to run up and punch him in the head because the rattle of that cart, was fuckin up my zone. I had never held a gun before, so I had to psyche myself out.

Two hours later, Ace elbowed me. Porter was walking out the club. I spotted him stepping in his Pimp Walk like he owned the city. We pulled our ski masks down over our faces.

Just as he was opening up the driver's door of his Cadillac, we was on his back. I pointed my Glock at his left temple.

"Empty them pockets!" I yelled.

"You mutha...." He started to say. Everything happened in a flash. Porter pushed me catching me off guard and then gun almost slipped out my hand. I squeezed the trigger shooting him in the face. The gunshot knocked him down on the black pavement, blood pouring from his face and he was screaming, "Oh God somebody, help!" For a split second, Porter became Larry and I pointed the Glock at his face. Ace grabbed my arm. "We out!" he yelled and I heard police sirens screaming a block away. We ran five blocks to the car.

"Nine better have our paper for this shit!" I ripped my ski mask off and my purple t-shirt. I noticed Porter's blood was splattered on the front. A chill ran down my spine but I didn't let Ace know that I was trippin out.

"He said lay low until he reach out. He about his business!" Ace stood up for his cousin. "I'ma pull over to a dumpster so we can ditch these clothes and the ski masks."

"Right on, right on!" I told him glad that shit was over.

Chapter 7

Bae Bae

"Boss, you need to take this call!" Blackboy shoved the phone to my ear.

"Who is it nigga?"

"Mac's wife!" He whispered

I reached for the phone. "Speak!"

"Is this Nine?"

"Who dis?"

"Bae Bae!"

"Where's Mac?"

"I buried him yesterday! Can we talk?"

"Meet me at The Flame, on Jefferson!"

"I know where it's at!"

"Be here in an hour!" I said and press the dial to hang up.

"What she say boss?" Blackboy asked me.

"Mac dead!"

Me and my uncle was sitting in the back booth across from each other discussing numbers for the restaurant.

Blackboy popped up on my side of the booth.

"She here!"

"Put that on pause Unc!"

"You want that money to keep rolling we gotta get these repairs done!"

"I got you!" I threw the words over my shoulder.

When I made it to the door, Hardrock was standing guard next this petite brown lady. She wore her hair pulled back in a ponytail. Her sky-blue sundress stopped at her knees. Her alert eyes watching everything in the room.

"Boss she said she Mac's wife!" Hardrock announced.

"How I know you ain't a Fed?" I asked her.

"Yo proof is in this envelope!"

She was quick with the tongue. I liked her immediately.

"Call Ms. CeCe in here!"

Blackboy ran to get her from the kitchen. Ms. CeCe was my part time spy. She kept a low profile but she always packed two pistols. She was my uncle's wife.

Ms. CeCe returned with Blackboy.

"Ms. CeCe take her in the back and search her. Blackboy you go with them."

"Hardrock go start up the ride!" I yelled not taking my eyes off her.

Hardrock disappeared to the back of the restaurant.

Five minutes later Ms. CeCe, Mac's wife, and Blackboy in the rear returned to the dining room.

"She clear!" Ms. CeCe reported then headed back to the kitchen.

I turned to Blackboy, "Tell Hardrock we going to the Furnace."

Blackboy followed Hardrock's path. Me and Mac's wife was alone.

"What's your name?"

"Are you Nine?"

"I'm asking the questions!"

"Everybody call me Bae Bae!"

"We going for a ride!" I told her pointing in the direction to the back of the restaurant.

At the Furnace we headed to the basement. Hardrock was outside standing guard. The basement was fully remodeled with a bar and a half bathroom.

"Have a seat!" I told her she was still clutching the manilla envelope.

She took a seat on the couch and I sat across from her in a lazy boy. Blackboy sat on a bar stool at the bar.

"Let me check out that envelope." She handed it over. I dumped the contents on the glass coffee table. Pictures of her and a smiling Mack and their three kids.

"Mack was a good dude. What happened?"

"Died of a heart attack." She said her voice choked up.

I reached into my pocket and pulled out five thousand dollars and handed the wad of money to her.

She put her hand up to stop me. "I don't want charity, I need a job!"

"Take it until you find something." I held the money out.

"Can you answer my question? She asked.

"Shoot?"

"Are you Nine?"

I nodded my head yes.

"I want Mack's job." She announced

"I ain't hiring!" Then I stood

She shot up from the couch. "Mack taught me everything! Unpacking, mixing, and weighing."

"Blackboy let's go!" I said

" I have three kids to feed. Gimme a couple of ounces of your purest stuff and I'll cook up some stones better than them ribs y'all got at the Flame!"

Bae Bae was not a fraud, she stepped into Chef Mac's shoes and made magic.

Chapter 8

Nine

One night we was cruising down highway 70 in Rasheed's Jeep. I was riding in the passenger side in deep thought about the old dude that I spotted every morning in my bakery peeping me. I knew he was a Fed. Me and my crew held it down so I kept telling myself not to trip he ain't seen nothing or heard shit.

"Get off at Broadway!" I told him.

"Where we headed?" he asked

"I need to think and the scenic route is what I need right now." I answered.

Rasheed exited the highway at Broadway.

I noticed people standing at the bus stop looking hot and sweating from the heat even though the sun was down. Then I noticed him shuffling down the corner of 9th street and Locust Ave.

"Pull over!" I shouted over the music blasting from Rasheed's radio. I knew that walk from anywhere. Rasheed pulled the Jeep over. I hopped out the Jeep and jogged until I caught up to him. I shook my head at the rags he was wearing. His shirt looked like torn up pieces of rags sewn together to make a shirt and his pants had big gaping holes at the knee and thighs. His shoes caked with dirt from sleeping on park benches and doorways.

"Dad!" I called out to him.

He kept walking.

"Dad! I raised my voice. He picked up his shuffling.

I had to be bold so I jumped in front of him and looked him dead in the eyes.

The eyes staring back at me was lifeless and glazed over.

"Dad it's me, Alex!" He gave me a blank stare and he moved his lips but no sound came from his mouth. The smell of piss and sewer made me want to throw up but this was my dad.

"How you been man?" I didn't wait for him to answer. I reached into my front pocket and pulled out a hundred-dollar bill and reached for his hand. Dad jumped back and held up his hands like he was surrendering to the police

"I ain't got nothin!" He mumbled his eyes blinking fast.

"No Dad! Here it's money." He snapped out of it at the mention of money.

I held his hand and slid the money onto his crusty palm then I turned to leave. I spotted Rasheed standing guard at the Jeep.

"LaDonna...!" I froze my steps and I turned towards Dad at the mention of my mother's name.

"LaDonna?"

The words I wanted to say to him stuck in my throat and my mind was swimming with memories of him teaching me how to play chess.

"I gotta go Dad! Take care of yourself." Then I broke into a jog running from the painful memories of losing my dad to PTSD and mental illness.

Chapter 9

Regrets

I started coming home late so I could avoid Larry and Mama especially when he started beating on her. Larry would start arguments with Mama and then he started telling me and Danny what we could and could not do. Just runnin shit!

A week after I shot Porter, I was relaxing at the crib. Nine told me and Ace to lay low. Mama had cooked a big dinner. Danny went to get more food out of the pot.

Larry told him, "You ain't gon keep going in that pot!"

We were all in the kitchen sitting at the table. It was me, Lil Michael, Danny, and drunk ass Larry. Momma was standing at the sink washing dishes.

I mean mugged Larry and said, "Nigga who you talkin to?"

Larry snapped his head around to face me, "I wasn't talking to yo ass but now I am!"

"Yeah, nigga and I'm talkin to you, now what?" I stood up to face him. He was only a few inches taller than me. Momma stood in the middle of us.

"Tell this lil nigga I ain't playin." Larry told Momma mean mugging me at the same time.

"Okay baby, calm down!" Momma said to him.

"Nigga you ain't my Daddy, get the fuck out, that's what!" I told him.

"Derrick watch yo mouth————-

"What? You gon take his side, Momma?"

"I'm not gon keep reminding you about being disrespectful. This my house!"

"This our house Momma! Not this muthafuckah!"

Momma slapped me. "I'm tired of you thinkin you grown!"

I walked away without saying a word. When I got to the bedroom, I started shoving some clothes in a duffle bag. Danny walked in. "Bro what you doing?"

"I'm gettin the fuck outta here!" I zipped the bag and stormed out of the bedroom.

When I opened the front door, Momma said, "Derrick it's seven o'clock at night get yo ass back in here!"

I kept going and slammed the door behind me. For two weeks I crashed at my cousin's apartment in the Cochran projects. Then I stayed Aunt Irene's house for the next two weeks. Her house was loud as the Greyhound station so I asked Ace if I could stay at his crib.

Two days later, me and Ace was standing outside The Flame, Nine's restaurant. We was able to walk in no bodyguards was blocking the door. Nine was sitting at a long table in the back like he was the mayor of this city. The place was empty but this time I smelled barbeque ribs cooking instead of bleach like the last time we met him.

I felt somebody walk behind us and it was a pecan brown older lady dressed in a white apron. She flipped the open sign to closed and then turned the locks on the door.

"Fellas whas good?"

"Just making it! Know what I mean, cuzzo?" Ace fired back.

"Here!" he reached into his pocket and pulled out a fat wad of cash. He peeled off five one-hundred-dollar bills handed them to Ace. Then he counted out five bills for me too.

"Word on the street, Porter looking like Freddie Krueger, he gon be laid up for a while!" Nine announced the hood news.

"That's a damn shame!" Ace said.

"I want y'all to holla at Boss Man." Nine announced. "Kick it with him for a minute!"

Boss Man was a top dog hustler, he ran the North Side. He was known for shutting down whole blocks to sell his dope. Nobody questioned him because him and his crew would make the hood rain bullets if anybody got in his way.

"What's a minute?" I asked him. Ace was smiling like a kid on Christmas but me I was thinking.

"A couple of weeks!" Nine said.

Then the pecan brown lady popped up from the kitchen carrying two platters piled high with barbeque ribs. She sat them down in the middle of the table. Next a bald-headed dude bought out another platter filled with potato salad and a pitcher of lemonade. The lady came back with two empty glasses. She slammed the glasses down, one next to Ace and the other one next to me and poured us both a glass of lemonade without saying a word.

I took a sip and tasted liquor mixed with the lemon.

"Eat up!" Nine said and walked away.

We watched Boss Man for two weeks. Ace did all the driving and I rode shotgun. Most of the time Boss Man drove from dope sets to local bars. I memorized the routes Boss Man drove when he was by himself. When he was rolling with his entourage it was two or three cars driving, one was in front of him and the other car trailed him.

One evening Ace, his girlfriend Tasha and my off and on girl Yolanda was posted up at his crib, we got a call from the streets. We was grooving to some music and a knock on the door put a pause on the mood. I turned down the volume on the radio. Ace answered from the couch, "Who is it?"

"Got a message!" a dude on the other side yelled.

Me and Ace reached for our straps.

"Speak!" Ace told him we both aiming our guns at the door ready.

"Union Station tomorrow matinee! The Return of Swamp Thing! Don't be late!" one of Nine's goons said.

"Understood!" Ace yelled then we heard him walk away.

"Man, whas up wit yo cousin? The Return of Swamp Thing?"

"Will you chill? Put that slow jam tape on so we can get it right up in here!" Ace grinned. I changed the tape from a mixed rap tape to a slow jam tape I made a week ago. Ace turned up the volume on the radio and we went back to smoking and kicking it with our girls.

The next day it was me, Ace, and Nine sitting in the back row of an empty movie theatre. Nine sat in the middle of me and Ace. He was wearing a gold watch that had diamonds on the face.

"Tell me...whas up wit my boy? Nine asked us in between smacking on popcorn.

I answered, "He top doggin' it."

"Yeah we been checking him out at some of the pool halls near his set." Ace backed me up.

"Check this, I think we followed him to one of his spots." I told Nine.

"Yeah, niggas was carrying AKs out of this house on Simple Ave. They even had duffel bags about ten of em." Ace said.

"That's fucked up...niggas start getting sloppy quick. It'll be a damn shame when we read about this fool takin a slug because some niggas got up on em and robbed em." Nine said.

Me and Ace digested his words. "He going to sleep?" Ace asked his cousin.

"Heard you got a shorty on the way? Five stacks will set up you real nice, cousin." Nine smiled.

"My girl always on me about getting a job." Ace said.

"You already got one. I don't like horror they a waste of my time. Peace my niggas." Nine said and bounced.

When we left the movie theatre the sun was still up. Sunlight burning my eyes I had to blink a couple of times, get my eyes right from the dark movie theatre to blazing sun.

"Aye let's hit the boxing gym." Ace spoke up.

"Yeah, that's what I need right about now." I spoke. "That shit Nine just laid on us got my head fucked up. I need to hit the bags!"

At the boxing gym I punched the hanging bag while my thoughts traveled back to the movie theatre and Nine's words rang in my head. I wanted to tell that fool that a 187 was not my thing. But the money!! Both me and Ace was waiting on this boxing thing to take off so we could hang up our ski masks and guns.

The bell rung for me to stop punching. My chest was going up and down while I tried to catch my breath. All I could do was watch the punching bag go back and forth as sweat dripped from my forehead.

"Two more rounds Derrick!" Coach shouted from across the gym. He was setting up the weights so me and Ace could weight train. Ace was on the side of the ring, jumping rope.

I threw my first punch at the bag, then I hit it again, each time my red boxing gloves hit the bag, I saw Boss Man's face and Nine's face.

On the way to the Jets, Ace said, "If we pull this off Nine would keep us on the payroll and we could stack mad cake and even buy a car."

"Man, I ain't down with killing nobody Ace!"

"Quit bitchin up!"

"You do realize and recognize what the fuck we about to do?" I asked Ace. A nervous feeling in my stomach.

"Ain't shit to me. Once it's done, he putting us on. We gon get money just to put niggas in check!" he threw two air punches like he was giving his opponent body shots to the torso.

Chapter 10

Nine
Queens of My Heart

"Mom! Alex here!"

I heard one of my sisters yelling as I put the key in the door to my mom's two-story red brick house. I bought the house for her when my bankroll got up to one million a week. One of the coldest houses on the block on Utah Avenue in Tower Grove Heights. Before buying the house, I made a promise to myself to move my Mama, my four sisters, and my daughter Ayanna to a two-bedroom apartment on Arsenal Avenue. When I got deep into the drug game, I made it my business to move them out of the Cochran projects.

"Son! We in here." I heard my Mama's voice

I headed to the family dining room. On the table, white porcelain platter plates held, waffles, fresh fruit, one of my favorites, potato broccoli egg casserole, bacon, sausage, country hash browns, a pitcher of fresh squeezed orange juice and a pot of coffee. Homemade cinnamon rolls posted up in the middle of the buffet of food. Mama sat at the head of the table. I kissed my Mama on her forehead then I took the chair next to her. My daughter Ayanna, we called her Yanna, was sitting next to me in the chair to my right. I greeted her with sign language, "Hi sweetheart." And she responded in sign, "Hi Daddy!" then she hugged me.

My daughter was born deaf. I was doing time in Bowling Green County, my first drug case, when she was born. Her mother Shauntay, left her at the hospital so my Mama went to get her. My Mama and my sisters took care of her from day one.

My four sisters, Salena "Lena" the second oldest under me was sixteen. She was tall, pecan brown, and slim and she was the hair stylist of the family. Then Tanisha "Nisha, she was fifteen, shorter than Lena, the fashion guru of the family and more hot headed and stubborn than me, then the two baby girls Leah who was twelve we called her "Lee Lee", and the youngest Michelle "Shelle" was eleven. They the reason why I went hard in the streets.

Lee Lee spoke up, "Mom, can we eat now?"

Mama looked over at me and said, "Alex say the grace, baby."

"Lord thank you for this food that you blessed us with this morning. Amen!"

"Amen! Mama and my sisters repeated.

After we ate, I helped clear the table and helped Mama wash the dishes.

"Son, you don't have to do this. Go sit down."

"Nah I'm good Mama."

"Whas wrong? Look like you got something on your heart?" Mama asked me.

"I think the Feds watching me!"

"Why you say that?" she asked rinsing a plate then handing it to me to put in the dishwasher.

"At the bakery, it's this old dude be watching me. I never seen him before. He there every morning. So, I laid low for a couple of days, didn't go but he come back when I'm there."

"He say anything?"

"Naw, I catch him staring at me every time I look up from my paper."

"Son, I know you don't want to hear this but...."

"Mama it's not time. I gotta provide for this family!"

"Son, you did your job. Now it's time for you to look out for yourself!"

Chapter 11

Regrets

As soon as night blanketed the city, me and Ace touched down on Robin Avenue. Ace was posted up two houses down hiding in the shadows both of us watching everything moving. I counted three niggas that went into the small shotgun house. Standing across the street in the gangway of two houses, I patted my waist for the fourth time, a nine-millimeter with the silencer was tucked in. When Boss Man pulled up in his white 98 Oldsmobile, we moved like ninjas silent and unseen. Within seconds, I was crouched behind his ride. Ace stood behind a huge tree that was in Boss Man's neighbor's yard.

The bass from Boss Man's car stereo blasted in my ears, he was bumping the rapper Too Short's number one jam back then, "The Ghetto." It took him awhile to get out the car after he parked. I could hear my heart thumping in my ears. A few minutes later, I heard the driver's door open.

"Get yo hands up nigga!" I stood a few feet back because I didn't want him to get up on me like Porter did.

"Robbing ass nigga. I'ma have to kill one tonight........" he held his hands up.

I slapped him in the back of his head with the gun. "Muthafuckah get to steppin!" My voice surprised me because I sounded different with the black bandana tied around my face.

He stumbled up the two steps that led to his house holding the back of his head. Ace sprung from the tree and followed us.

"Get them muthafuckas to open the door!"

"Open up I forgot my key it's Boss!" the Lil nigga sounded hard. I heard the locks on the door turning. The door opened and I shoved Boss Man inside knocking the dude off his feet. Ace grabbed Boss Man and gave him a hard blow to the side of his face with his Glock. Blood squirted all over Boss Man's jogging suit.

I spotted one of Boss Man's soldiers sitting at a large glass dining room table bagging up stones. Dude reached for his gun, I shot his ass in the leg. "Awww!" he screamed.

Ace stood over Boss Man, his 9-millimeter pointed at him.

"Where the other nigga at?" I asked the clown I just shot.

"Man, ain't nobody else here, take the dope and the money it's all on tha table!" the dude begged.

"I'm runnin this shit not yo soft ass. Now where the other nigga at?" Ace yelled, "Behind you!"

I turned around in time to see the third dude charging at me with a knife in his hand. Ducking him I landed a body shot to the right side of his torso. He was caught off guard but he kept swinging the knife at me. I hit him across the face with my nine-millimeter and he crumpled to the floor like a piece of tissue paper.

"Get the shit!" I told Ace pointing my gun to the table with the stacks of money and Ziploc bags of dope.

I switched places with Ace and stood over Boss Man. He started crawling on his stomach. "Bitch quit moving!"

"Awight man! Just take what you want man, I got kids!"

"Listen to this mufuckah crying like a bitch." I laughed. Ace was stuffing a duffle bag that sat on the table with the drugs and money.

I kicked Boss Man in the ass. "Yeah, how that shit feel niggah? You ain't so tough now!" Two weeks before when we was watching Boss Man, we saw him kick a woman in her butt. She was begging him for dope.

The dude I knocked out tried to stand up so I raised my gun and filled his torso up with three bullet holes. His body crashed to the floor with a loud thud. Boss Man's eyes got big as saucers and he tried to get up and run.

"Nigga do it look like I'm playing with you?" I yelled at him.

"Man please. I ain't ready to die."

I pulled out my second nine-millimeter and shot Boss Man with both guns in my hands. Two shots to his head and two to his torso. Half of his face splattered on the floor.

Ace turned around and shot the dude laying by the table in his head killing him instantly.

We jetted out of the back door and into the dark alley. The alley was deserted but we still kept our weapons close and our eyes and ears alert to anything moving. The runaway car a 1981 Buick Skylark was parked three blocks away. I jumped behind the wheel and Ace rode shotgun.

I drove from St. Louis Avenue and Marcus to 21st street and St. Louis Avenue and parked the car in an alley. Ace popped the trunk, then he pulled out a can of gasoline and poured some in the inside and outside of the car. He lit a match and flames exploded everywhere licking the air and dancing.

On foot we headed back towards the projects. Before we reached the Jets, we changed our clothes throwing away the clothes and the bandanas into a dumpster then Ace set the dumpster on fire. I felt relief when Ace burnt the car up and our clothes because the memory of Boss Man and his crew burned in the fires.

"Ace why the fuck you still carrying that bag? Burn that shit!"

"Chill Legend. I'ma give this dope to Nine, man! Show him he fucking wit some real killas."

"Fuck that dope selling muthafuckah. We stuck to the script and that's all that nigga get. Fuck is wrong wit you?"

"Come on man Nine is fam." Ace threw up his hands.

"Dumb ass nigga you know I don't fuck wit dope. I don't want that shit around me!"

"Legend chill. We almost at the Jets"

"When we get there, I'm shaking yo stupid ass."

After that night the nightmares came.

"Y'all niggas be easy and don't trick all yo money off."

Me and Ace sat across from Nine. It took him a month to pay us for the Boss Man job. He called us to meet him at The Flame. One of Nine's waitresses delivered two white plastic bags to Me and Ace. Each bag had a white Styrofoam food box stuffed inside.

"Y'all niggas be easy and don't trick all yo money off."

I wanted to snatch the glass he was sipping from and slap it across his face. I hated when drug dealers talked shit.

"I got something for you, fam!" Ace smirked and grabbed the black duffel bag he stole from Boss Man's dope house and pushed it across the table to Nine. Nine unzipped the bag peeked inside and nodded his head.

"I'ma be in touch wit y'all cats." Nine stood up clutching the duffle bag in his right hand. He disappeared into the kitchen.

"Let's get outta here." I told Ace.

Once we was outside, we headed for the alley to open the food boxes. Inside each box was stacks of hundred-dollar bills. We stuffed the bills in our pockets and tossed the bags into the dumpster.

I hadn't stepped foot in my Mama's house for a month. My pockets was heavy from the stack that Nine paid me. I unlocked the front door using my key, I braced myself for Mama to start yelling and Larry sitting on the couch sipping a forty but the house was quiet. I spotted Danny sitting on the couch with a long face.

"Fuck wrong wit you?" I sat next to him.

"I'm cool." Danny wouldn't look at me.

I knew something was up. "Where Mama?" I asked.

"At work."

"Where that nigga at?" I leaned back watching my little bro.

"He gone." He stared down at the floor. Then Michael ran into the room.

"Come here Lil bro!" I said. Michael put his hand out for me to give him five so I slapped him five. Then I reached into my pocket and pulled out a twenty and slid it into his small hand.

"Thanks man."

"You welcome Lil Bruh."

"Can you give Danny one too, that man took his money and we couldn't get no chips!" Michael looked all serious.

"You mean Larry?" My eyes bounced from Danny to Michael.

"No! The man at the store!" Michael blurted out.

"Danny what happened?"

"That old nigga that work there said I was a smart mouth muthafuckah and to get out his store, he ain't giving me shit back!" He frowned.

"What you say to em?"

"He told me to hurry up I was looking at the chips, I told him to shut the fuck up and then he told me to get out his store. I asked him to give me my money, then he said, "It's my money now! Get the fuck out my store!"

"He don't own shit, them Arabs own it and he a nigga runnin around in it. Fuck that let's go!" I said. Michael didn't have no shoes on so I told him, "Michael go put yo shoes on man."

He ran to the bedroom and threw his shoes on. I said, "Let's go."

The store was a five-minute walk from our apartment. I walked into the dingy ass store first, then Danny, then Michael. The man was bagging up a customer's six pack of beer. We stood quietly waiting on his scrunchy ass. The customer held a cane, he took a quick peek at us and limped out the store.

"You owe my brother some money." I looked him dead in his eyes."Man y'all lil niggas get on up out my store with that bullshit!"

"Nigga do I look like I'm bullshitting?" I wasn't backing down.

He came from around the counter, he was sporting a salt and pepper fro. He stood at 6'2, I was 6 feet. He stood in front of me.

"Get the fuck outtah here before I throw y'all project asses out!"

"Nigga don't run up!" I told him then he swung on me. My boxing skills took over, I ducked then punched him in the gut with a right hook knocking him to the dirty rotted wood floor. A lady and two teenage girls was about to step into the store but the sight of him on his butt and me standing over him with my fist balled up, the lady screamed and ran from the store but the girls stayed to watch the show. He tried to get back up but I pulled out my pistol and slapped him across the face with it. Blood squirted out of his nose spraying on the floor and the ice cream cooler. I saw Larry's face again and I kept hitting with blows to the face until his eyes was closed and he was no longer moving. Out of breath I put my pistol back in my waist and said, "Bitch ass nigga!" then I kicked in his backside and his back.

The girls ran into the store snatching chips and candy and then blasted out the store.

Danny and Michael was silent as we walked away from the store.

"Where you get that gun?" Danny spoke up.

Then one of the girls ran up to us and she made eye contact with me. I was happy she ran up because I didn't know what to tell Danny.

"You put it down on his ass, he a mean muthafuckah." the girl was light skinned with sandy brown hair and very skinny. Her white tennis shoes was more yellow than white.

"I'm Candy, me and my sisters stay on Maffit, the corner apartments." She smiled at me.

"Candy?" one of the other girls called for her.

"Awight now!" I said then she ran off to join her sisters. I knew I wouldn't give her the time of day. She looked like an overgrown pee pee kid.

Lil Michael and Danny was silent as we walked to another corner store. This store was bigger, they had more liquor and more aisles of chips and snacks.

"Get whatevah y'all want!" I told them. I snatched up a forty ounce of Coors beer, Danny and my Lil bro piled up bags of chips and candy and soda on the counter next to my forty ounce.

The man behind the counter was a young dude from the hood. He said, "You know I can't let you walk outta of here with this." I pointed to the forty ounce. I slid him an extra twenty-dollar bill. He snatched it up and rung up the snacks and packed them in a paper bag.

Chapter 12

Regrets

"Derrick where you been? It's eleven o'clock and you just now walking in my house?" Mama stood in the middle of the hallway with her hands on her hips.

I kept walking to my bedroom. Mama followed me. I could feel her footsteps inches away from the heels on my tennis shoes.

"Boy, don't you walk away when I'm talking to you!"

I turned around to face her. "I'm here now so why you trippin?"

"You been drinking?" she stepped back like the alcohol smacked her in the face.

"Will you stop sweating me?" I was ready to hit the bed. Me and Ace was hitting the Hennesy and chased it with weed.

"Who the hell you talkin to?"

"Larry fucks up all the time but you treat his ass like he King Vitamin———-"

"Larry is not my sixteen-year-old son."

"I'm going to bed." I tried to turn around but she stopped me.

"You not going to bed until I'm done talking. You ain't runnin shit in here."

"Where Larry at? Hunh Mama?"

"This ain't about Larry."

I peeped Danny standing at the bedroom door.

Mama yelled to him, "Go back to bed Danny boy."

"I'm not putting up with you no more Derrick. Get your stuff and leave my house."

"You gon put me out but let that crack head ass nigga stay?"

"Get yo stuff and get out!"

"Cool I'ma leave." I walked pass her and Danny and into the bedroom. I snatched my duffle bag out the closet. Mama followed me into the room.

"Don't pack nothin I bought you. Ya hear me?"

"Mama you ain't bought nothin since Larry moved in."

"Hurry up Derrick." She folded her arms.

"Why I gotta leave, why you not putting Larry out?"

"When you pay a bill around here youngsta that's when you can talk shit!" Larry popped up in the doorway.

"Larry baby I got this." Mama said patting his chest.

"Man, who the fuck you talkin to?"

"Derrick watch yo mouth."

"Fuck that nigga, he ain't my daddy."

A wicked laugh came from Larry.

"I'm done talking to you Derrick!"

"Aw, so I'm the villain around here Mama? I say some cuss words but this bum smokin crack, stealing the VCR and TV———-

"You ain't no damn angel boy,"

"You ain't been an angel either Mama!"

"What?"

I walked up to Danny because he didn't listen to Mama, he stood in the doorway.

"Danny? Big Rick ain't dead. Mama been lying all these years. Our daddy in the pen for life."

Mama's eyes got big and out of nowhere her palm smacked my face. She got up in my face gritting her teeth, "You keep yo damn mouth shut."

The front door opened and she shot to the living room, "Larry where you going?" she screamed.

"Out!" then the front door slammed shut.

Mama stopped in front of me in the hallway. "Who told you?"

"Uncle Harold."

"Go to bed." She whispered then she disappeared down the hallway to her bedroom.

Two weeks before Thanksgiving, I was home chilling with Mama, Danny, and Lil Michael. Nine told me and Ace to lay low after the Boss Man murder. Larry walked through the door drunk. He started arguing with Mama then stumbled into our bedroom.

He yelled, "Cut that shit off I don't work to pay a goddamn electric bill."

I jumped up and got in his face, "Fuck you, my Mama pay the bills nigga!"

"Get the hell out my house you hoodlum!" the smell of whiskey floating from his mouth and pores attacked my nostrils and my throat. "Get yo drunk stank ass away from me!"

Mama walked into the bedroom, "Derrick! Don't use that gutter talk in my house."

"Mama, you hear how this drunk stepped to me?"

"If you can't do what I tell you then get out!" she screamed.

"Fuck it then!" I ran to the closet snatched up my backpack.

"Did you say fuck me?" Mama asked.

"No Mama, I said. Just forget it I'm outta here." I slung my backpack over my shoulder and left the house. Halfway down the block, I heard Danny yelling my name, "Derrick!"

I froze as Danny ran towards me. Out of breath Danny blurted out, "I wanna roll wit you!"

I hesitated glancing in the direction of our house. I was expecting Mama to come running after Danny at any second. When she didn't pop up, I told him, "Come on! we out!"

I led the way to the boxing gym downtown. We walked for one and a half hours and only stopped once to buy snacks and soda pop. Danny did flinch a bit. Once we made it to the gym, it was pitch black dark inside. I didn't spot Coach Green's Mini-van, I was able to relax a bit but I still had to be on point in case somebody was still inside.

I whispered to Danny, "Be quiet don't say shit, and stand behind me."

I stood in front of the back door listening for movement or voices inside. I reached inside my backpack for my lock pick. In one swift motion the door was open.

"Stay here." I told Danny. I tiptoed around the gym and it was vacant. I went back to get Danny and I was out done by Lil bro, he waited quiet and didn't ask too many damn questions.

We set up camp on the side of the boxing ring.

"Why didn't we hit the Jets?" Danny asked.

By then we was chilling eating chips and cookies that we grabbed from the liquor store.

"We gon be peaceful right here." I told him.

I kept the truth from him. I didn't want to tell him that I avoided the Jets that night because our Daddy's side of the family lived in the Cochran Projects and if Mama wanted to come looking for us, they would definitely spill the truth about where we were posted up.

We left the gym before the sun came up and posted up at Ace's house. Ace lived on the other side of the Cochran opposite where our Daddy's side lived. And I did everything to keep us out of sight because I digged having my Lil bro around. We stayed at Ace's house for two days because his mom worked as a live in nurse during the week. Ace went to stay with his girl so me and Danny had the apartment to ourselves.

One morning as we was leaving the Jets Danny asked, "So we going back home?"

"You wanna keep thugging or you ready to go back to the crib?"

"I wanna roll with you big bro."

"First thing, today you gon learn how to shoot." We was headed down an alley. I pulled out my Glock from my waist and handed it to Danny. He held the gun like he was a natural, he didn't flinch instead he aimed it at the dumpster. I smiled on the inside. Later that night we walked to a vacant field downtown near the Arch. Just under some bridges, I taught Danny how to aim and shoot. After I let him shoot, I showed him how to pull the clip out the 9-millimeter and change the bullets.

That night we ended up sleeping on Aunt Irene's couches.

Chapter 13

Regrets
December 1986

"What did you do?" Mama's screamed. I still held the shotgun in my hand. When the bullets from my gun sliced through his right temple, Larry's body went limp. Mama ran to his lifeless body and cradled him like he was a newborn.

This shit went down quick as lighting. "Mama!" I didn't hear Danny walk into the living room. Mama glared at me while she held Larry's dead body, blood oozing out of his temple and onto her white buttoned-down shirt. I couldn't believe she was holding this fool like he was a Saint. Larry beat her ass every day of the week and twice on Sundays. She laid his body down on the couch, jumped up and came at me like a fierce tornado.

Mama kept punching me in the chest and head but I stood there taking it. When her fist got tired, she started kicking me. "You ain't shit! You ain't shit!"

"Mama!" I cried. "Larry can't hurt you no more!"

"Larry! Larry!" she screamed then fell to her knees.

Danny tried to help her up but she pushed him away and she ran to the telephone.

I looked at Danny with fear in my heart. "She calling the police on me! Mama?"

She ignored me and kept punching the numbers on the mustard yellow telephone that was mounted on the living room wall.

"Mama! Stop!" Danny yelled. Lil Michael our baby brother was balled up underneath the kitchen table.

Thinking fast I dashed out the house. Ice cold wind slapping my face and ears. The rain was mixed with ice that night. Tuning out the small icy pellets hitting my face I kept running, my feet hitting the slippery sidewalk. I almost tripped over an empty fifty-ounce beer bottle. I walked and ran to the Cochran projects where I knew I would be safe.

Chapter 14

Not My People

After Mama slammed the phone down, Derrick got ghost from the house. Larry's eyes was wide open starring at the ceiling. Mama cradled him in her arms like he was her baby.

"I'm sorry! I'm sorry!" she repeated rocking back and forth.

"Mama!" I yelled but she ignored me.

I reached for Lil Michael and put his coat on. I was wearing a hoodie and two t shirts underneath because the house was always cold. Larry didn't like Mama to turn up the heat in the house. I scooped Lil Michael up and ran walked two blocks to Aunt Irene's house. Lil Michael was little but his body felt like a ton of bricks. By the time we reached her porch, the rain had penetrated my clothes. I was shivering from the wet and cold.

"Danny what you doing out in this rain, boy?" Uncle Rufus yelled when he opened the front door and noticed me and Lil Michael standing on the porch.

He opened the door and I ran into the house. I put Lil Michael down.

"Auntie! Auntie!" she ran from the kitchen.

"What's wrong?" Aunt Irene stepped from the kitchen, she was wearing a white apron and her hands was coated in flour. I could smell chicken frying.

"Derrick...Larry's dead!" Everything else was a blur. I woke up hours later on the couch, my cousins J.D., Casey, Cory, Lil Man Man, and Quinton sitting on the living room floor waiting on me to open my eyes.

Aunt Irene had six kids, Quinton her oldest, we called him "Q", Lamont his nickname was Lil Man Man, Jeffrey Dorrell, we called him

"J.D.", the twins, Casey and Cory, and the youngest Candice, we called her "Candy Cane."

"Where's Lil Michael?" I sat up.

"Man, you passed out!" J.D. said he gave me a serious look.

"Go tell Mama Danny woke up." Quinton told all of them.

Casey hopped up and ran to tell Aunt Irene.

"Where's Lil Michael?" I asked my heart racing.

"He in Mama's room sleep." Quinton told me.

I covered my eyes because I wanted this to be a nightmare so I could wake up.

The cops took Mama. They kept her at the police station all night drilling her about what happened. The next day a plain cop car dropped Mama off at Aunt Irene's house. Mama laid in bed all day sick with grief and Aunt Irene took care of her, Lil Michael, me and my bad ass cousins.

Tired of being in the house, me, J.D., Casey and Cory went outside to play football in the street. It was on a Thursday afternoon. Five minutes into the game, two cop cars and a plain grey four door Pontiac rolled up and parked outside of Aunt Irene's house. My stomach felt like it dropped. I prayed that Derrick was still alive. Me and my cousins raced into the house.

J.D. yelled to Aunt Irene, "Mama, the police here. You think they killed Derrick?"

I wanted to punch his ass for saying that about my brother.

"Boy hush!" Aunt Irene told him. Then the police knocked hard on the glass screen door.

"Ya'll get downstairs!" Aunt Irene waved her arm toward the basement. J.D., Casey, and Cory disappeared but I know they was at the top of the stairs ear hustling. Quinton didn't move, he stood next to Aunt Irene. He was sixteen, same age as Derrick and he stood at 6'3. I spotted my Mama sitting on the couch wearing pink house shoes and one of Aunt Irene's robes, that was two sizes too big.

Aunt Irene opened the door. The cops stood on the porch and a white lady that was 4'11 and blond stepped into the living room. She was dressed in a navy-blue skirt suit. She stood in the middle of the living room hugging a manila folder.

"Hello Mrs. Gates!" her voice was tiny.

"Hello!" Mama's voice was scratchy.

"Is this Danny or Michael?" the lady asked Mama.

"What you want?" Mama checked her.

"My sister been through enough, now get on with it so she can rest!" Aunt Irene spoke up as if she was going to body slam the lady.

"I have a court order stating that Danny and Michael will be place in temporary foster care until a thorough investigation has been completed."

"What the hell they investigating?" Aunt Irene yelled at the woman.

The blond woman didn't flinch. "The murder——-" she started to explain then the front door opened and a Black woman walked in. She was tall and brown sported a Sunday school teacher smile. Her hair was pulled back into a bun and she wore glasses, the frames too big for her face.

"Hello!" big glasses spoke she was nervous.

"This is Mrs. Hall and she's going to take Michael to his temporary home, and I will be placing Danny."

"You separating them?" tears was streaking Mama's cheeks. I wanted to kill Larry twice for putting me, my Mama, and my brothers through this bullshit.

"I'm afraid we have no choice, the foster homes are full————"

"Can they stay with me?" Aunt Irene asked.

"Are you a registered foster parent with the state of Missouri?" blond asked.

"I'm his blood, his aunt!"

"I'm sorry you would have to file a request with DCFS."

Lil Michael ran into the living room and sat next to Mama. His wild eyes was staring at the strangers.

"It's time we have to go." Blond said in a flat tone.

Mrs. Hall reached for Lil Michael and he kicked her in her leg and screamed, "Noooo, Mama, I'm not leaving!"

Blond got up in my face and said, "Danny let's go!"

I ignored her and went over to Michael. I hugged him. "Stop crying man it's gon be okay. It's gon be me, you, and Derrick. You can go everywhere with us."

"Everywhere?" Michael asked still crying.

"Yeah man, I promise."

He hugged Mama and she held him tight. Aunt Irene snatched me up in a hug. "I love you nephew. We ain't gon leave you and your brother to strangers, okay baby?"

Rage held my tongue. I wouldn't take my eyes off the front door.

Mrs. Hall took Lil Michael's hand and they left the house.

Blond started for the door and I followed behind her, then Mama called me, "Danny boy?"

I didn't turn around, "Yes Mama!"

"Son, come give me a hug." I turned and walked back to the couch and hugged my Mama but I wouldn't look at her or Aunt Irene.

"I love you!" she said.

"Love you too, Mama!"

When we reached to the porch, I spotted Mrs. Hall driving off with Michael in the back seat of a white minivan.

Aunt Irene, Quinton, JD, Casey, and Cory piled on the porch and watched blonde steal me away from the family. I rode shot gun in her grey Buick century.

"What grade are you in Danny?"

I ignored her.

"Do you like sports?" As she rambled, I checked out how the city changed from two to four family apartment flats to houses with green lawns that looked like carpet. It was barely any sidewalks and the houses were far apart. There was no corner liquor stores just grocery stores with clean parking lots and shiny new cars parked perfect. I studied the street names, Halls ferry Blvd, West Florissant Blvd, Chambers Ave. I had never heard of any of these streets. All I knew was the Cochran projects and North St. Louis.

She turned on a quiet street with one story houses lined up on both sides of the street.

"We're here." She said like we was on a game show and she was giving me a prize.

I wanted to say, "Bitch I know you parked the car, didn't you?"

We both got out the car and I followed her as she walked up this long walkway with small shrubs. She pressed the doorbell. I heard a television blasting on the other side and kids laughing.

The door swung open and an old Black woman was standing there. Her lips was black like all she did was suck down cigarettes. And her hair stood straight up like she been electrocuted.

Blonde gave her a fake ass smile. "Hello Margaret."

"Come on in." the lady named Margaret shot back.

Once we was inside the house, I noticed two boys younger than Michael playing with match box cars in the living room.

"This is Danny." Blonde introduced me.

"Hello." Ms. Margaret said.

"Hey." I spoke then I felt somebody staring at me. A fine ass light brown honey was standing in the doorway in between the living room and kitchen. I couldn't take my eyes off her.

"Danny!" Blonde called me.

"Yeah?"

"I'll be making a home visit next week!"

"Yeah whatever!" I told her ready for her to get out my face. She left out the front door quick as lighting.

"Come on I'll show you where you sleeping!" Margaret said.

I looked back at the girl and I noticed that she was checking me out, too.

Ms. Margaret showed me the bedroom. I had to share with the two young boys.

"Let me tell you my house rules, boy!"

I stood there.

"Don't go in my kitchen after dinner. You eat what's on yo plate or you go to bed hungry."

"Can I call my Mama?"

"Phone off limits, you hungry?"

I shook my head yeah. I wanted Mama or Aunt Irene's cooking because this lady looked like she couldn't cook.

"Kim this Danny!" Margaret said when we got back in the kitchen.

"I know, I got ears." Kim snapped her up. She was standing at the sink washing dishes.

I sat down at the kitchen table.

"Did you put the food up?" Ms. Margaret asked Kim.

"It's in the refrigerator!"

"Get it out and fix him something to eat!" Margaret barked and left us in the kitchen.

Kim dried her hands on the dish towel and opened the refrigerator. She pulled out two pots and slammed them on the counter then she turned her pretty ass face towards me and rolled her eyes as she opened the cabinet and grabbed me a plate.

"Girl you better stop slamming shit in my kitchen before I knock yo ass out!" Margaret yelled from the living room.

"How old are you?" she asked me then she slammed a plate down in front of me.

"Old enough." I told her.

"You got a smart-ass mouth." She said and smiled at me. I didn't smile back.

She scooped some Mac n cheese out of one pot and she took out pieces of fried chicken out the second pot. Then she popped my plate in the microwave. After my food warmed up, she sat my plate in front of me then handed me a fork.

"Thank you." I said.

"Don't get used to this shit." She glared at me.

At eight o'clock, Margaret made us go to bed. I wouldn't sleep. An hour later she went to bed and I went to Kim's bedroom. I knocked a couple of times then she opened up the door wearing a Looney Tunes nightgown.

"Where's the phone?" I asked her.

"Ms. Margaret keeps it in her bedroom."

That was a blow. So, I stood there thinking how was I going to call my cousins and my Mama?

"You can get your ass on now."

"Girl ain't nobody looking at you!" I headed back to my room.

The next day Margaret enrolled me in school. The first thing I noticed was a Bi-State bus driving away. Instantly, my mind wondered how far did it travel? Hopefully to the North side. When I walked into class, all the kids stared at me like I was an alien. What was fucked up was all the Black kids talked and acted white. I barely listened to the teacher all I could think about was running away from Margaret's house.

Later that evening Ms. Margaret left the house to take the twins to their weekly visitation with their Mama. Kim was in her bedroom with the door shut. As soon as, Ms. Margaret drove off, I raced to her bedroom door. I turned the knob praying that it wasn't locked and to my surprise it opened. I did a quick sweep with my eyes and I spotted the red phone sitting on the night stand.

The dial tone was music to my ears. I dialed Aunt Irene's house, my heart beating wild.

One the third ring, Lil Man Man answered, "Hello!"

"Lil Man Man this Danny. Put JD or Casey on the phone!"

"Casey ain't here, man where you at?"

"I ain't got time right now but I'll tell you later. Put JD on the phone."

"Hold on." I heard him sit the phone down.

My hands got sweaty as I listened for any noises outside Ms. Margaret's bedroom.

"Who dis?" JD finally made it to the phone.

"This Danny."

"Where they take you?"

"I'm at some old lady's house. You heard of some streets called Halls ferry or Chambers?"

"Naw nigga that sound far."

"Shit I'm tryin to get up outta here."

"I'ma ask some of the OGs about those streets, say the names again?"

"Nigga Halls ferry and Chambers."

"Awight when you gon call again?"

"As soon as I can, I gotta go."

I couldn't get to the phone for a week. Ms. Margaret guarded the telephone like it was gold. And on top of that she never left the house. One day after school, as soon as I crossed the front door, she told me, "Keep yo coat on we headed out!"

We hopped in the car and she drove forever. I paid extra attention to the street signs so when I rapped with JD I could tell him. She parked at this beige building and I spotted Mama standing outside. I jumped out the car and ran to her, she hugged me so tight.

"Where's Michael?" I asked her.

"Let's go inside, baby." Mama was wearing her blue waitress uniform and one of Larry's winter coats. Seeing Mama in his coat made my skin crawl. She wouldn't let him go after he was dead.

Inside I glanced around, it reminded me of the Welfare office except it was not yelling angry women and long lines and crying babies. And it was couches and tables with chairs. Ms. Margaret took a seat on one of the couches in the back of the room watching and ear hustling on me and Mama's conversation.

"I saw Michael yesterday and he's fine. He's at Annie Malone." Annie Malone was a children's home.

"What! Mama you gotta do something——-

"I am Danny, baby just be patient. How you doing?"

"Where's Derrick Mama? They still looking for him?"

"Look!" Mama jabbed her finger at me. "He ain't my concern. My only concern is you and Lil Michael."

Mama's coldness towards Derek pierced my heart and rage took over me.

"Danny boy! Derrick is the reason why we in this mess don't feel sorry for him."

I looked away and I didn't respond.

"Danny boy, behave yourself. Don't give these people any problems."

I wouldn't take my eyes off the white wall."

"Boy you better answer me when I'm talking to you!"

"Yes Ma'am." I tucked away my pain.

"Danny! Look at me when I'm talking to you."

I glanced up and saw my brother's eyes. Mama passed down her honey brown eyes to Derrick.

"I love you, son."

"Love you too Mama." Then she grabbed my head with both hands and kissed me on the forehead and smiled. Even though she smiled, sadness filled her eyes. At that moment, Mama looked dwarfed in that coat. Her body looked frail.

On the ride home, thoughts of my brothers and my Mama clouded my mind. When we got back to the house, Kim was sitting on the couch with the twins' watching cartoons.

"What's up?" she spoke.

Angry at the world, I ignored her and the twins and went to the bedroom. All evening, I sat on my bed plotting on how I was gon run away. I ignored them when they called me to the kitchen to eat dinner.

Two hours later, eight o'clock it was lights out for everybody. I had just dozed off, then I felt the other side of my bed move. I laid still then I felt an arm wrap around my back and stomach and soft lips on my neck. I turned around and Kim was smiling all up in my face.

"What you doing?" I whispered I didn't want to wake the twins up or Ms. Margaret. She pressed her lips on mines and slid her hand down my boxer shorts and squeezed my Johnson.

"Ouuu, you packing." She whispered stroking me with her hand.

My body was in flames. I had never kissed a girl. The only girl I wanted to hit was Gigi.

"Come to my room." She said and crawled out my bed and floated out the door.

I followed her and once we was in her bedroom she ripped off my t-shirt and my boxers.

We ended up naked in her bed and she climbed on top of me and took over.

A week later, Ms. Margaret and Kim left me at home with the twins to go grocery shopping. As soon as, I heard Ms. Margaret's tires rolling down the driveway, I flew to her bedroom. Once I was in there, I spotted the red telephone. I dialed Aunt Irene's telephone number. Nobody answered so I hung up waited a few seconds then redialed the number. It rung five times then Casey answered.

"Casey man, is JD there?"

"Whas up?" Casey asked me. I could hear a Marvin Gaye song blasting in the background.

"Trying to get up outta here."

"JD told me what's up. We got you."

"Straight?"

"Yeah nigga! Let me go get em." I heard Casey throw the phone down.

"What up D?" JD picked up.

"Tell me whas poppin."

"The big homie Ant said he can swoop you but you gotta meet us at Halls ferry and West Florissant. That nigga said he got warrants and he ain't driving deep into the county. So, when you wanna do this?"

"Tomorrow!" I told him.

"Awight Im'a tell Ant tonight."

"What time?" My heart was racing because I was gon see my family soon.

"What's good for you?"

"Shit, um ten."

"Damn, ten?" JD asked

"Yeah, I gotta play it off. The old lady drops me off at school at 8:15. So I'ma leave the school and then I gotta walk Hella far to get to y'all niggas."

"Awight."

"Good lookin out!" I told him.

"Fuck you nigga, you know we got yo back."

Chapter 15

Regrets

For a week, I slept in that vacant apartment. One of the families we grew up with, moved to the South Side and the apartment had been vacant for months. I survived off potato chips and sandwiches. When the sun went down, I curled up with my gun every night., One night, I got restless so I left the Jets. As I jogged, I breathed in the fresh cold night. I ended up at Laclede's Landing near the riverfront. My stomach started churning, I hadn't eaten since the night before. The lights from the McDonald's boat twinkled down the road. My hands started shaking as I gave the lady my food order. I handed her my last twenty-dollar bill.

I sat in the back of the restaurant out of sight. As I wolfed down the Big Mac and fries, I kept my eyes on the window expecting to see the waves in the Mississippi but all I could see was darkness. After I finished my food, I walked around on the deck. The smell of rotten vegetation from the river made me hold in my breath for a minute to escape the stink. I reached for my Glock and tossed it into the river. My heart sank when I heard the splash. My gun was my best friend. I went back to the Jets and the vacant apartment. The next night, I hit the alleys, the less I was on the street I wouldn't get spotted by cops or snitching ass niggas. I ended up at one of Nine's trap houses on Simple Avenue. It was a row of four family flats and Nine snatched up two of them. I hid on the back porch of an abandoned house until I could get my head together. When I got the nerve up, I headed to Nine's spot. A stray black and white cat jumped on the top of the roof of an old car that had a broken wind shield and two flat tires.

"Who dat?" one of Nine's soldiers answered. The block was quiet and the lights in the street lamps was broken.

"Legend!" I answered. My heart was beating in my ears and my stomach was in knots because I wasn't sure if they knew I was on the run.

The dude opened the door. "Sup Legend." It was Rasheed one of Nine's Lieutenants.

We hit each other with a dap. My body was sucking up the heat blasting from the vents in the wall. "I need to holla at Nine."

"He be around this way in a minute." Rasheed said.

"Can I chill until he get here?" I didn't want to return to the cold.

"Yeah man, take a seat."

I noticed Nine's other Lieutenant, Black Boy. He mean mugged Rasheed while putting rubber bands around stacks of money.

"What?" Rasheed asked. "It's cold as hell out there Black. You want the man to get frost bite?"

"It's cool, I'll holla at Nine later." I said and left up out that piece.

Three blocks away from the trap house, my stomach rumbled. I was weak and tired from hunger. I felt some headlights on my back so I ran, the frigid wind slapping my face and ears. When I picked up speed, I slipped and fell on black ice. My hands hit the frozen concrete. I heard tires screeching. I reached for my gun, then I remembered it was at the bottom of the river.

"Legend?" the voice sounded familiar so I froze then turned my body.

"Nine!" my chest burning from inhaling the cold and I was out of breath.

"Nigga what you doing out here in this hawk?" He had the passenger window down. That night he was pushing his gold Range Rover.

"I need to holla at you!" I told him.

"Jump in." Nine was sporting a tan skull cap and fresh Timberland boots.

His truck was presidential, plush leather seats and an expensive sound system.

"Whas good?"

I heard him but I was thawing out and hunger pains stabbed my stomach. All I could do was stare at the street signs as the truck glided down the block.

"Legend?"

I jumped. "My bad, umm..."

"Nigga you high?" he asked.

"Fuck naw, I need some cash, boss. You know I'm good for it."

"When this cold thaw out, I'm putting you niggas back to work."

"We got you boss. Can you drop me off at 18th street?" We said nothing else during the drive.

Once we hit Tucker Ave, I told him, "Pull over, I can walk from here."

I looked out the window checking the streets, I spotted a couple of bums shuffling in the cold searching for a warm place to sleep for the night.

Nine pulled over, parked then reached in his pocket and pulled out a wad of bills and handed me all of them.

"Big ups for having my back." I told him then hopped out the truck. The wind slicing through my coat. I gave one of the bums twenty dollars to go into the gas station to get me some food and I let him keep the change.

Once he came back with the food, I jogged to the boxing gym. All the lights were out. But that didn't mean nothing. Coach could still be in his office watching old boxing tapes of some of the boxers he trained back in the day so I listened for any movement or sound. The night cold was so mean that it shook my arms and legs.

I looked around for something heavy like a rock but I found an empty beer bottle and stood back a few feet from the door and threw it at the door. No sound. I waited a few more minutes and remembered I didn't have my back pack, it had my lock picking tool in it. If I had my Glock, I would have shot that damn lock open. I kicked at a brick, stomping my frustrations out on it, then I snatched it up and hurled it at the glass door knocking a chunk of glass out and shattering it at the same time. I looked around for witnesses but the street was quiet except for the sound of the wind and the drizzle of rain dancing on the pavement.

Inside the gym, it was pitch black dark. I ripped down a poster of a heavy weight boxer who made it to the pros. Then I went to coach's office turned on the light and ram shackled the drawers in his desk until I found some duct tape. I taped the poster over the hole in the door.

Even though, it was inky black in the gym and the workout equipment from the punching bags to the weights looked like shadows lurking in the darkness, I felt safe.

I climbed into the boxing ring, and peeled off my damp hoodie and hung it over the ropes. My eye lids got heavy and sleep took over. Hours later hunger pains stabbed my gut, I knew I had to leave before the sun came up. Ace's house was the next stop. It was risky but I had no gun and no food. If Ace could give me a few more hundreds, I had planned to add that to the money Nine gave me and then I could hop on a Greyhound and get out of St. Louis.

At 3:30 am, I walked into the Cochran projects. I kept reminding myself, "Look no one in the face." The army green jacket, I found in Coach's office kept me warm. I wore it over my hoodie and I kept my hood over my head. Out of nowhere, I spotted flashing red lights, I thought it was the hunger and cold making me crazy. When I heard tires screeching and engines revving up my stomach dropped.

"Freeze!"

I didn't move but inside my head I told myself, "Just run...run into the building...you know the inside like the back of yo hand."

"Turn around! Slow!" the police officer barked.

I took off. "Yeah, I'ma make it, they can't fade the Legend!"

At four feet from the door, one of the officers tackled me like we was on a football field.

Chapter 16

Back in tha Hood

Ms. Margaret dropped me off in front of the school. I walked into the building, waited for her to drive off then I dipped out. I walked down Halls ferry Ave for an hour almost freezing to death in the December cold. I made it to West Florissant Rd. I scanned the parking lots and the strip malls and I didn't spot anybody from the hood. I inspected each car that drove past me, when I started losing hope, I heard a car horn blowing. I looked toward the sound and I saw a sky blue 1975 Nova pull into the Ventures parking lot. The big homie Ant, was behind the wheel and JD was riding on the passenger side. Ant was in his thirties, a tall light skinned dude with a short Geri curl. To us, he was an old head back then. He used to be in the Army but when he came home all he did was stay in his Mama basement and collect his Veteran check. He would pay us to steal cartons of cigarettes and whatever else we could get our hands on.

When I got to the car, Ant jumped out the car and pushed the driver's seat forward so I could climb in. The engine on the Nova was loud like a diesel engine. I stepped into the back seat and empty aluminum cans crushed beneath my feet. The heat from the car vents blasting.

"Man watch my cans!" Ant yelled over the sound of the engine. Ant peeled off into the busy West Florissant Ave traffic and we headed for the hood.

JD filled me in on all the happenings in the hood as Ant drove. Ant dropped us off two blocks from Aunt Irene's house.

"OG, I got you!" I told Ant when we got out the car. I gave him some dap and so did JD. Ant speed off.

Me and JD walked the alley so no one would see us. When we reached Aunt Irene's house, we went in through the basement door. Music was blasting through the door.

"Hold up, who in there?" I stopped in my tracks.

"It's cool, man chill." JD pushed the door opened and all of my cousins was posted up in the basement. Quinton was sitting on the couch chilling, Casey was switching a cassette tape on the boom box for another one from the stack of cassette tapes, Cory and Lil Man Man was sitting on the steps that lead to the upstairs hallway.

"D? Whas up cuz?" Casey yelled. I slapped all of them five.

"Aye Lil Man Man go get the cooler!" Quinton told him.

Lil Man Man ran over to the other side of the basement and came back dragging a red cooler.

"We got something to tell you D." When Quinton talked everybody shut up. "Casey turned that down." Quinton ordered.

My mind started racing.

"Derrick got picked up this morning." Cory who rarely talked spoke up. My heart sanked. I hung my head because my eyes started burning as I held back the tears.

"Here cuz!" JD spoke up handing me a cold bottle of beer. I took the beer and sipped it slow. Everybody reached into the cooler and grabbed a beer and gulped it down like it was water.

"How y'all niggas cop these?" I asked feeling stronger after a buzz hit me.

"Lil Man Man got em." Casey said

"Yeah cuz, I knew you was coming home today so I went shopping." Lil Man Man was only ten years old and everybody knew his shopping was stealing from one of the corner stores.

"Damn they got my brother." I stared at the yellow liquid inside the beer bottle.

"Now you home D, we can all go see him." Lil Man Man spoke up.

I wished I was home for good. I knew Ms. Margaret found out that I didn't show up for school and I ran away. But none of that shit was important to me, I had to figure out a way to see my brother.

For the rest of the night, we had our own party in the basement. JD bought out the dice. Once the game got started, we was on our third bottle of beer. Then Casey popped open the Mad Dog. I was drunk by the time when the dice game was over. JD and Casey told me all the news that was going on in the hood. Who got shot and who went to jail. At 2am we shut it down.

"Lil Man Man go upstairs and see what's going on." Quinton told him. He came back in three minutes. "Man it's packed up there. I'ma stay up there because I know one of them drunk fools is gon drop some bread out they pocket." Lil Man Man said.

"Where's Mama?" JD asked.

"She in the kitchen." Lil Man Man reported

"Go talk to her, keep her in there while we get D upstairs." Casey said.

My head was spinning. I had to rest my head in my hands.

Lil Man Man raced up the stairs.

"Nigga you drunk?" Casey asked me.

I couldn't speak, my tongue felt heavy.

"D, you awight man?" JD asked me.

"I'm good."

"Let's go before Mama walk out the kitchen." Casey said. Casey took the lead up the steps then JD, me, then Quinton.

The next morning, I was dreaming about me and my brother running from the police. I heard Mama's voice booming from the sky. "Danny boy!" Derrick was in front of me running. Two policemen was closing in on us. "Bro keep going don't stop!" I yelled to Derrick's back then him and the police disappeared.

"Danny! Wake up!" I felt the covers being snatched from me. "Danny!" I opened my eyes and Mama was standing on the side of the bed with her hands on her hips, dressed in her blue waitress uniform.

"Mama?" I sat up but my head felt like it was filled with concrete.

"Boy get yo ass up and get dressed."

"Mama I just woke up, I'm tired."

"Why you leave that foster home? If you sat yo ass down you could still be sleep."

"Mama, I don't like being at that house, that lady crazy————"

"Get yo ass up, I ain't gon tell you again."

I climbed out the bed headed for the bathroom but Mama grabbed my arm.

"Don't do this shit no more Danny."

I yanked my arm away from her. "Do what Mama? I ain't did shit. All I wanna do is see my brother." She slapped me so hard I saw white stars floating.

"You will never see his no-good ass!" I was so embarrassed to get bitch slapped by Mama in front of my cousins.

I threw water on my face then rinsed my mouth next, I threw on my clothes.

Mama was waiting for me in the hallway. She walked down the steps when she spotted me coming out the bedroom. "I don't know why you and Derrick think y'all my Daddy. I'm the damn Mama. If you wanna be like yo stupid ass brother, you gon end up locked up just like him. And I'ma have one child to think about!"

Chapter 17

Regrets

I sat in the courtroom next to my court appointed attorney. I kept turning my head around to see if anyone from my family showed up, but I didn't spot any familiar faces. The judge gave out sentences like Halloween candy, to the other juvenile inmates standing in front of me wearing orange jumpsuits and metal bracelets. Danny and Lil Michael flashed in my mind. Now that I was locked up, I hoped Danny would raise up and be the man of the house. Teach Lil Michael about the streets.

"The city of St. Louis versus Derrick Gates!" the bailiff announced.

My attorney touched my right shoulder to stand up. *I thought to myself, Time to put on my gorilla face like I don't give a damn!* I could feel the other juvenile delinquents and the on lookers in the courtroom staring at my back.

"Derrick Gates! You are being charged with murder in the second degree. How do you plead?"

"Not guilty!" My voice shocked me. I hadn't spoken since they hunted me down.

"Your honor there was no murder weapon found when my client was apprehended."

Yeah, that's right, it's at the bottom of the Mississippi River. I should have stayed at that trap house and they would have never found me but I had to keep running....

The other cracker on the state's side stood up, "We have a sworn testimony from the mother your honor, she witnessed the defendant shooting and killing the victim Larry————"

"That's right lock his ass up!" a lady sitting in the back of the courtroom shouted.

I turned around to put a face with the voice. We had never met any of Larry's people.

"That muthafuckah shot my brother down like a dog!"

"Order!" the judge slammed down the mallet. The lady in the back stopped yelling but her cries stabbed my ears.

"The defendant is 16 years old and the people is requesting a certification hearing to try him as an adult, your honor." The prosecuting attorney cracker spoke up.

"Certification hearing is granted." The judge shuffled some papers.

"The hearing is scheduled for November 4th. Court is adjourned." The judge slammed down his mallet.

My legs became Jello, as I stood up. I felt like I was in a bad dream.

Chapter 18

Nine

One week before Christmas, I met a potential soldier from Memphis. Black Boy and Hard Rock had my back. We met at the St. Louis Centre in the food court. This cat said he had $50,000 to spend with me. They called him Rebel. One of my cousins from Memphis worked with him a couple of years back. We met at 1:00 pm. He was sharp and he had his paper so the deal went smooth. Rasheed was waiting with the product. Black Boy took the money and put it in one of the safes in one of my houses.

I left the mall, Hardrock keeping in step with me.

"Hey boss! I waited till the meeting was done to tell you that they picked ya boy up!"

"Who?" My steps slowed down.

"Legend! Got him for smoking his Mama's old man."

"Oh yeah!" I said my mind digesting what Hardrock just revealed to me.

"You think he gon start snitching?" he asked me.

"Keep ya ear to the streets and if he do, his Mama gon be bending over his casket cause we gon kill his ass!"

The sky turned from sky blue to dark grey and the wind picked up. It felt like the temperature dipped. I reached for the door to go into Famous N Barr to buy Mama the roasted peanuts and jelly beans she loved.

"Alex!" My arm stopped midair when her voice kissed my ear. I turned around.

"Shauntay?"

The snow started floating from the grey sky. I felt like I was in a scene in a Christmas movie. Christmas music buzzing in my ears and the outside store decorations sparkling.

"How...how you been?" Damn she was still beautiful. Shauntay my ex. Her Mom was white and her Daddy was Black. She had that creamy smooth skin. Her ebony hair was cut short. Black curls falling on her forehead.

"I'm good." I said playing it off. I wanted to kiss her perfect face then take a razor and carve lines into her cheeks.

"How's Ayanna?" Her eyes was full of desperation. She was hungry for more info but I let her starve.

"Fine." I gave her the death stare for bringing up our daughter that she abandoned in the hospital when she was a newborn. I was locked up when she had Ayanna. The doctors told her that something was wrong with our baby. Turned out Ayanna was deaf and she had a hole in her heart. My daughter had to have three surgeries and my Mama went to the hospital to pick up my daughter and we had her every since.

"Doing some early Christmas shopping?" she asked.

"Yeah, I gotta hook my girls up."

"Look at all those bags you carrying, you must be tired." Her smile was evil. And her sarcasm was like a knife twisting in my back. "Shopping my ass, you working. Once a criminal always a criminal!"

"And misery is so yo style shortie. Peace!" I stepped off and left her ass standing on the sidewalk.

Chapter 19

Regrets

On February 15, 1987, I was in the courtroom again for my sentencing. They certified me as an adult. I scanned the courtroom searching for Mama, anybody from my family. Every wooden bench in the courtroom was packed. I spotted Larry's sister.

"All rise!" the Bailiff announced.

The judge walked in, "Please be seated!" he shuffled some papers then he called my name, "Derrick Gates!"

I stood up.

"By the city of St. Louis in division 18 court, you have been found guilty of second-degree murder. As of February 15, 1987 you are sentenced to a maximum of ten years without the possibility of parole."

"That's some bullshit!" I heard a man's voice behind me. Then I felt a punch in the back of my head knocking me into my attorney and the wood table. Papers and folders flying everywhere. I tried to fight back but three dudes started stomping and punching me in my face and stomach. Five bailiffs rushed into the courtroom to pull the dudes off of me.

Chapter 20

Regrets
One Year Later...

On my eighteenth birthday, February 12, 1988, the guards showed up at my cell to transport me to the adult male prison. It was 2:00 am. They put a belly chain around me and cuffed my hands and feet. Two guards walked me out to the prison van. The icy wind cut thru my jail issued coat. Inside the van was ten adult males and the driver. One guard sat in the back cradling a semi-automatic pistol.

When we made it to the prison, I soaked in my new surroundings. I spotted young men and men my Daddy's age.

"Fresh ass!" An old dude with salt and pepper hair blew a kiss at me. After intake, they took me to my cell. My roommate was a slim light skinned cat that wore pointy glasses. He wore a knitted cap on top of his head.

He looked up from his book and said, "Top bunk."

Chapter 21

Home

It was a year and a half later when the Child Welfare people sent me and Michael back to my mom's. The morning, I was leaving, I was expecting Mama and Aunt Irene to pick me up but the case worker showed up. My stomach dropped when I spotted her stepping up the walkway in black high heels.

When Ms. Margaret let her in, she looked at me and said, "Danny! You ready?" I answered her by picking up my bags and running out the house not looking back. I was mad because I had to finish 8th grade without my cousins plus Kim left six months before me because her grandmother finally got custody of her.

When the caseworker pulled up to our new apartment building, Mama, Lil Michael, Casey, Corey, and JD was standing on the porch. Mama moved two blocks over from where we used to live before Derrick killed Larry. It felt good to be back in the hood.

That same night me, JD, Cory and Casey was back to our hustle but instead of snatching and running we broke into liquor stores in the middle of the night.

One night I got home at eleven o'clock at night and Mama was slumped over on the kitchen table. Her plate of spaghetti untouched. Lil Michael was asleep on the top bunk of our bedroom.

I shook Mama's right shoulder.

"Mama!" You a 'wight!"

"What? It's time for me to get ready for work!" Her words slammed into each other.

"Mama! It's night time."

Her eyes shut closed and she put her head back on the table. Her arms a pillow. I scooped her up in my arms and carried her to bed.

A month later we started ninth grade at Sumner High School.

The first day at Sumner High I peeped all the players. It was the Polo boys and the 49 street cats. All of em was hustlers. The Polo boys rocked short sleeve Polo shirts with the starch collar and jeans and fresh Nikes but everybody started calling them dope man Nikes because the Polo boys rocked em. The 49 block cats wore white t shirts and jeans and K Swiss.

Then I spotted GG at her locker. For the first time I was scared to step up to her because I was rocking my cousin JD's clothes. Money was tight at home. Mama worked two jobs but our lights was always getting shut off and we didn't have a house phone.

She was standing with Tracy at her locker holding two books in her arms. Her thick black hair flowed past her shoulders. She was laughing at something Tracy was saying.

"Sup GG!"

"Damn Danny you fine! You done grew up!" Tracy loud mouth ass said.

"Tracy you still the same."

"Boy shut up gimme a hug." She laughed.

I gave her a side hug.

"You tall now!" Tracy said.

GG hugged me with one arm. "I didn't think I was gon ever see you!"

The bell rung.

"GG let's go we gon be late!" Tracy bossy ass said.

GG wouldn't move it was like she was waiting on me to say something.

"Walk me home after school?" She asked.

"I'll find you." I told her. She smiled and turned around to walk with Tracy.

Chapter 22

Not Good Enough

I caught up with GG after school. She was walking with her other friend Sky and her sister Queen. Sky and Queen was nicknamed pee pee kids since Turner Middle. They would show up to school wearing dirty clothes and smelling like piss. GG was the only one that would talk to them.

That day a foul smell wasn't attacking my nose. They clothes wasn't dirty but what they wore was faded hand me downs.

"Told you I'll find you."

"See y'all tomorrow." She told Sky and Queen.

Then we was alone walking down Newstead Avenue. I felt like I was in a dream walking with the girl I spent plenty of nights dreaming about. I leaned in close and GG's hair smelled like cocoa butter.

"Why you hang with them?" I asked her.

"Danny don't tell me what to do. Sky and Queen are my girls."

"Are you gon be my girl?"

She stopped walking and stared at me.

"If you gon be cheating and lying to me and trying to tell me what to do then hell No!"

"Come on GG. You know I'm that nig...fuck that.... I been feeling you since the 6th grade?"

"Boy come on. It's hot and I'm hungry." She hooked her arm around mines and started walking.

When we turned on Cottage Ave, GG's house was the first house next to a duplex. Her Mama was getting groceries out the trunk of their car. She let go of my arm and moved away from me.

"Shit! Mama wasn't supposed to be here!" she whispered.

Her mother disappeared into the house then came back out. Shed stood on the porch watching us like a hawk.

"My Mama work nights. Can you come over later?"

"What time?"

"Ten!"

"That's too damn late!"

"Hi Mama!" GG's voice was sweet and innocent when she spoke to her Mama.

"Get in this house Goddess!" her Mama put her hands on her hip. Seemed like a dark cloud was passing over her face when she looked at me.

"What's wrong Mama?"

"You!" GG's Mama pointed at me from the porch. "You from that family that live on Cote Brilliant?"

She was talking about Aunt Irene's house but I said, "Yes Ma'am!"

"You stay away from my daughter, don't come around here no more or I'm calling the police!"

"Mama?" GG begged.

I didn't say shit cause nobody was gon keep me away from my girl not even her Mama. When I turned my back, I heard their front door slam shut it pierced my spirit but I shook it off.

Chapter 23

Mama

When I got to my block, the ambulance was parked outside our apartment building. I spotted Aunt Irene holding Michael's hand and Mama being wheeled on a stretcher. I ran as fast as I could before they pushed Mama into the ambulance.

I felt somebody grab me from behind. "Baby? Calm down!" I recognized Aunt Zelda's voice.

My voice cracked. "What happened to my Mama?"

Aunt Irene spoke up, "She passed out! Thank God you was there with her sister!" she told Aunt Zelda. "Danny you and Michael go with Zelda, I'ma ride in the ambulance with Berenise."

In a flash, Aunt Irene and Mama was in the ambulance and it was speeding away.

"Go pack you and your brother's stuff, y'all coming with me." My mind started racing because all I could see was that blond case worker pulling up in that Buick Century driving me back to foster care. Ms. Margaret's cigarette smelling house! I vowed to myself at that second that I was gon run away and hide just like Derrick did before they put the cuffs on him.

"Auntie I'ma stay here." I told her. She gave me that look like I was disrespecting her. There was no way I was going to Aunt Zelda's house. My Auntie had six small kids and with me and my brother it would be eight under one roof. "In case Mama need me!" I cleaned it up.

"Okay but I'ma take Michael with me. I'm only two blocks away if you need anything."

"Yes Ma'am!"

I wasn't alone for that long. My cousins showed up, Casey, JD, Corey, and Quinton. We posted up in the apartment kicking it every day. I didn't go to school but they did. Every day I waited by the phone for Aunt Irene to call me to let me know when I could visit my Mama.

"Gigi been asking about you!" JD told me one day after school. I hadn't been in two weeks. I was waiting for Mama to come home from the hospital.

Aunt Irene finally let me visit her in the hospital. Mama looked like a rag doll in that hospital bed. She asked for some water so I pushed the button and she was sitting half way up. I handed her a white plastic cup full of water and her hand was shaking so bad that the water spilled all over her gown. I wanted to run and never come back.

" I'ma go up to the school tomorrow and catch her on her way to the crib."

"You need to bring yo ass to school." Casey said

"True."

So the next day I popped up at school feeling out of place. I ended up bouncing when I found out Gigi wasn't at school. At ten o'clock that night, I got dressed. JD and Casey was in the kitchen playing CDs on Casey's boom box and frying chicken.

"Where you going?" Casey asked

" Going to see my girl!"

"At ten o'clock at night? You a fool?"

"Stay out my bidness!"

"A 'wight you missing out on these wings and fries!" JD said.

"I'm out!" I said and stepped out into the night feeling strong ready to see my girl.

When I got to Gigi's house the porch light was on.

I walked around back staying out the light and I tapped on the storm door and waited for Gigi to answer.

I felt a shadow to my left and then I heard a male voice.

"Git yo ass away from here!"

I turned around and noticed a man with a rifle pointed at me.

I put both my hands up, "I'm looking for my boy Ant." I told him.

"You a goddamn lie. You better start running before I put a bullet in yo head!"

I backed away keeping my eyes on him until I was back in the street then I ran home. Derrick's face flashed in my head. If he was here, he would have handled that shit.

"Fuck wrong wit you?" Casey asked me he was standing at the stove frying chicken.

"Damn that was fast. You back already?" JD asked then took a swig of his forty ounce. I snatched it out of his hand and took a long as drink.

"Gigi's Pops held a gun at my head. I'm kinda fucked up right now!"

"Let's roll down on em!" Casey said.

"And end up like my brother nah!"

"Aye I heard it's going down at Skate King this Friday after the football game, we should check it out!" JD said smiling. "You know it's gon be packed wall to wall with fine ass honeys!"

"Yeah and you can leave that Gigi shit where it's at. Get you a real dime piece!"

"Fuck it we going!" I said but really, I was playing myself because Gigi was all I wanted.

Chapter 24

Roll like a King

Friday evening, we rode in Corey's mud brown Maverick. Corey drove, JD rode shotgun, and me and Casey hopped in the backseat. I wanted to duck down in the back seat cause I was embarrassed to be seen riding in that thing. After years of working on it in Aunt Irene's backyard he got it running and he drove that piece of junk like it was a Rolls Royce. The Skate King lot was packed with cars. I spotted a silver Range Rover and a midnight black BMW parked in front of the door and two big hulk hogan looking dudes on guard.

We heard the music as soon as we stepped out the Maverick. Jam on it was blasting and the DJ was yelling over the music. When we stepped inside, I felt like a bum. All the cats from Sumner was dressed. I peeped two dudes from the Polo boys on my left skating with two shorties.

The rink was full of life couples holding hands as they rolled around the rink. Skate crews dressed in matching outfits battling with they best moves. Lights was flashing from the ceiling.

The music filled up the place. And weed smoke mixed with hot dogs stung my nose.

Then to my right was a red rope blocking off a section for a birthday party. Balloons was on the tables and presents wrapped neat in birthday wrap. Two dudes was standing guard and I saw this cat wearing a gold nugget watch he was sitting at the table with the presents and four cute ass girls look like they was his daughters was smiling and laughing as an older lady snapped a picture of them with a Polaroid.

I kept my eye on them even while walking around the rink chatting up different crews.

"What up?" Chance said. His grandmother lived on Marcus Ave and he would spend Summers on the North side until school started back in September then he went back to live with his Dad in Spanish Lake.

"Aye who that dude in the VIP with the body guards?" I asked him.

"That's Nine!" He said. Chance wore a gold rope chain and a white shirt sleeve Polo and jeans.

"You down with the Polo boys now?" JD asked what I was thinking.

"Yeah I'm down." Chance said. He claimed North Side even if his address was suburb.

"Nigga you don't go to Sumner! How that happen?" JD kept going.

"Who this Nine cat? What's his game?" I asked. The Polo boys was a bunch of fake ass pretty boys. I wanted to know about the cat that had the bodyguards like he was a politician.

"Man y'all fools live on the North side and don't know shit!" Chance said. " He feed the hood, top dog in the dope game and he got real businesses."

"He the man we need to see." I said

"Dope ain't our lane Danny. We gon stay away from that shit." JD said.

"Let's get on some of these fine ass honeys." Casey said and they got lost in the crowd. I hung back plotting on how I could meet Nine. I knew that being with a real crew could change my life.

When I was about to join Casey and JD, I spotted Nine's bodyguards walking towards the door. Nine and the woman and the four girls with him was walking in between the guards. One of the girls was staring at me then she smiled and gave me a small wave when nobody was looking. Lil ass girl. I turned my head back towards the rink dance floor.

I was heated because I couldn't get that close. The guards stepped like they was ready to take heads off if anybody got within a foot of Nine and his family.

Chapter 25

Eviction Notice

It had been three weeks and Mama was still in the hospital. One afternoon I was in the living room falling asleep on the couch when I heard somebody taping something on our front door. I peeped out the window and spotted a dude racing down the steps and he hopped into a white 98 and sped off.

I opened the front door and saw a white paper with bold black letters, EVICTION NOTICE! A ten day notice to vacate the premises!

My mind flashed back to the skating rink and Nine. I had to do something to get some cash quick.

Kory and Casey knocked on the back door. I checked the clock on the kitchen counter and it read three o'clock. Every day after school they came over.

"Where's JD?" I asked.

"Went to Tracey's pad." Casey said opening the fridge.

"Thought they broke up?" I said

"They ain't no more." Corey said.

"Was Gigi at school?" I asked

"Nah! Forget about her!" Casey said "Her Daddy almost blew yo head off!"

"I need to talk to her. What about Skye she been to school?" I asked

"Her sister was there but she wasn't."

Corey said sitting at the table.

Casey said making sandwiches.

"I wonder do anybody have they number?" I said thinking out loud.

"Why you tryna push up on her dirty tail?" Casey asked

"He tryna get to Gigi!" Corey said.

"I know where she lives." Corey spoke up

"Where?" I asked hope speeding up my heart

"How you know where they live Corey?"

Casey asked.

"They live in those apartments off Kings highway and St. Louis Avenue.
"

"How they going to Sumner and they live all the way over there?" Casey asked in between bites.

"Bump all that let's go!" I said.

Kory fired up the Maverick and we rode over to Skye and Queen's apartment. When Kory turned onto St. Louis Avenue, I asked Casey about Nine.

"Where that cat Nine be holding up?"

"Man, Chance said Nine a Killah. Don't nobody want smoke wit him." Casey said.

Kory spoke up, "He be on that St. Ferdinand dope set."

"That's murder Ville!" Casey said.

We pulled up to Skye's apartment building.

I shut the conversation down about Nine.

When we climbed out the Maverick, I saw two Lil dudes about the age of Lil Michael sitting on their bikes.

"Hey y'all know Skye?" I asked

"Yeah why?" The skinny one with the buck tooth spoke up.

Casey pulled out two dollars and handed them to him.

His eyes got wide and he snatched them up. "I show you, her door."

I was behind the kid when we stepped into the dark building. It was no lights in sight. A person woulda though it was night time until they stepped out into broad daylight. The kid ran up the steps, I was tailing him, Kory behind me, and Casey the last one.

Candy wrappers and cigarette butts crushed under my worn-out Nikes. The steps creaked as we climbed up to the second floor. The stink of stale cigarette smoke and sweat hit the back of my throat I held my breath.

The Lil dude knocked on the door. I heard footsteps on the other side.

"Who is it?" A female voice asked

"Danny!" I spoke up. The locks on the door clicked open. Queen was peeking behind the door.

"What you doing here?" Queen asked

I wanted to say, "Not here to see you!"

But I kept my cool.

"Skye here?"

"Wait a minute" She slammed the door in our faces. I was about to turn around and leave then the door swung open.

Skye appeared at the door barely opening it. She squeezed out shutting it so we couldn't peep inside.

I got right to it, "I need you to call Gigi for me!"

She eyed me, Kory, Casey and Lil dude.

"We ain't got no phone." She said

"We can call her from the pay phone. You got her number right?"

"Be right back." She said then disappeared inside the apartment.

We piled back into Kory's ride and he drove to the payphone a block away.

Me and Skye climbed out the backseat. Standing at the payphone I handed her a quarter. She dialed Gigi's number. She looked at me and I turned away like I was watching the traffic on Kings highway.

"Gigi?" Skye said into the black phone.

I held my hand out for her to pass it to me.

"Gigi?"

"Who is this?" Her voice sounded so sweet.

"Danny!"

"Sorry Daddy pulled a gun out on you."

"I'm tryna see you. Come to my house."

"I can come after school tomorrow."

"Ima be waiting."

She giggled. I gave her my address then I hung up.

"Skye you a 'wight wit me."

I gave her dap.

The next day Gigi was standing on my porch knocking on the door.

I told Casey, JD, and Kory not to pop up cause my girl was coming over.

I let her in and she put her arms around my neck and pressed her body up against mines. Her skin and her hair smelled like Cocoa butter.

I couldn't take it so I swept her up and went to my mom's bedroom. I got the room ready before she showed up.

I rocked her body. It was her first time so I took it slow until I opened her legs and went in deep.

"You coming to school tomorrow?"

"I got a lot going on."

"Danny you can't keep doing this."

"A 'wight girl I be there for you."

"I better get home my Mama will be looking for me."

I walked her to her block then went back to my pad. I had to change the sheets because I noticed blood from where Gigi's hips was.

The next day I showed up for school. Every time we walked down the hallway, I held her close to let everybody know she was officially mines. I skipped my 4th period class to eat lunch with her.

At the end of the day, I walked her to the block then I headed to my spot.

As soon as I turned the corner, what I spotted almost bought me to my knees. All of our furniture, clothes, everything we owned was tossed out on the curb.

Kory and Casey helped me snatch up clothes and whatever else we could carry. Under a pile of broken plywood, I spotted Derrick's duffle bag. Casey was reaching for it but I pushed him away.

"Watch out that's my brother's shit!"

"Look D!" Kory was holding up a letter. I noticed my brother's handwriting.

"Where you find it?" I asked him

"Under that pile of mail!" He pointed to junk mail and bills.

Uncle Rufus and Aunt Irene pulled up in a loud ass beat up orange pickup truck.

Chapter 26

Montell Bey

It was Quinton, Casey, JD, and me walking down the hallway at Sumner High. We was leaving class period 2 on our way to period 3, we met up because all of our classes was in the same hallway.

"Dope man, dope man, yeah that's me, yo can I get a G, who am I?" Casey was rapping NWA's latest song.

"Tha dope man!" JD finished the lyrics.

I noticed Gigi a few feet away from me talking to somebody and she was all smiles. I couldn't see who it was because other people was walking past rushing to their classes. As I got closer, I saw that it was Montell Bey was all up in her face. He was wearing a burgundy and white letterman jacket.

"There go yo woman." Quinton said.

I didn't comment cause in my head I was asking myself, "Why she laughing all up in his face?"

Then Montell started whispering in Gigi's ear and then he slid his hand down her back and too close to her butt. I started walking faster leaving my cousins in the wind. I pushed Montell so hard he almost lost his balance but his books and notebooks flew out his right arm and onto the hallway floor flying in different directions.

"Damn nigga!" Montell yelled

In a silent rage, I punched Montell in the nose and it became a blood fountain squirting everywhere. His hands flew to his nose. I picked his ass up and slammed him to the floor. A crowd was around us everybody ignoring the late bell. I was on top of him pounding his face with blows from my fist. Two of Montell's football teammates, Romey, a quarterback and Brandon pushed through the crowd. Romey started punching me knocking me down. Casey jumped on Romey's 250 frame and JD grabbed Brandon by the neck.

Kevin was the head security guard at the school, a short nigga standing at 5'7 with a fat stomach and walked slow like a turtle but on that day, he was quick on his feet. Mr. Garner, the principal popped up to help Kevin break up the fight. Kevin grabbed me, but I pushed him off me and he almost fell on his ass.

Montell grabbed me by the neck and was choking me. Security guards pulled us apart. One of the guards pulled my arms behind me. Montell got away and punched me in the stomach and my side.

Mr. Garner grabbed Montell. Montell screamed, "Let me go!"

"Calm down Monty and I'll let you go!"

One of the guards handcuffed me and we started walking towards the office when Kevin tried to put the cuffs on JD.

"Don't touch my brother muthafuckah!" Casey yelled and ran up on Kevin. One of the guards grabbed Casey and body slammed him then he slapped the cuffs on him.

As soon as the principal was gone, Kevin said to the other security guards, "Take they asses to the office and call the police. I'ma have they asses locked up!"

One of the security guards dropped me off to Mr. Garner's office. I didn't know where they took Casey and JD. When Mr. Garner walked into his office, he stared at me like I was a caged animal ready to strike. He sat on the edge of his desk facing me.

"Wanna tell me what happened?"

I looked at his ass and said, "Man get these cuffs off me they tight as a muthfuckah!"

"Language?" he said.

"Man fuck, I wanna get the fuck outta here. What y'all gon do call 5'0 or what?"

"Danny tell me what happened?"

"Nigga was talkin shit."

Kevin walked in and stopped at the doorway looked at me frowned up and then asked Mr. Garner, "So how you want me to handle this Mr. G?"

"I can take it from here Kevin, uncuff him."

Kevin walked over to me snatched up my wrist then uncuffed me. I gave him a death stare so that nigga could remember me.

Before he left Mr. Garner's office, he asked him, "What you want me to do with the other two?"

"Uncuff them and keep em in the conference room, I'm calling their parents to pick them up."

A half an hour later, I heard Aunt Irene's voice, "I'm here to pick up my boys!"

One of the guards bought in Casey and JD, Aunt Irene walking in behind them. Mr. Garner said behind his desk.

"What the hell happened?" Aunt Irene put her hands on her hips.

"Jeffrey, Casey, and Danny got into an altercation this morning and caused quite a disturbance so I'm suspending them for the rest of the week."

"Bring y'all asses on. Got me ridin up here for some dumb shit!" she yelled everybody in the office staring at us.

On the way out the office, Uncle Rufus was standing at the door wearing a lime green suit. When we got outside, JD said, "Mama we can walk home!"

Aunt Irene turned around so fast to smack JD but he was quick and she ended up slapping the air. "Get ya asses in this car!" so we climbed into Uncle Rufus's tan 1972 Eldorado. We climbed into the back seat. Aunt Irene sat up front with Uncle Rufus.

"Lord, I hope I didn't miss Norman. That's gon fuck up my tripe party!" Aunt Irene said then turned around to face us. "Y'all better pray to Jesus that I don't miss the meat man cause I'ma beat some raw ass if I did!"

Norman was the neighborhood meat man. He would drive around the hood in his white truck selling pork steaks, fish, steaks, and chicken. Once a month, he would make a special trip for Aunt Irene. She was one of his best customers. Everybody in the hood knew Aunt Irene could fry the best tripe in town. Whenever she cooked tripe her card party guest list would triple.

"Mama! It was Danny's fault." JD spoke up pointing to me.

"Danny?" Aunt Irene looked at me.

"Yeah Mama. He started fu————"

Aunt Irene looked from me to JD.

"I mean he started punching this nigga and then the nigga's friends jumped Danny, me and Casey was getting them niggas offa Danny."

"Like I said, y'all better not fuck up my party." She turned around in her seat to look out the window. Uncle Rufus slowed down and parked his long ass ride in front of Aunt Irene's house.

As soon as we walked into the house, Aunt Irene yelled, "Clara? Clara?" Aunt Irene's friend Clara would sometimes help her cook for the big card parties. Clara was sitting in the living room watching soap operas on Aunt Irene's floor model TV.

"Did Norman come by?" Aunt Irene asked. My stomach knotted up waiting for Clara to answer.

"Not yet Irene!" Clara answered. I breathe and relaxed even though my body was sore from the fight.

Aunt Irene turned around to walk into the kitchen, Casey was standing behind her. She jumped.

"Mama I'm hungry." He told her.

Me and JD was sitting on the couch.

"Get outta my face." Aunt Irene told Casey then she headed to the kitchen. I went to the kitchen to get me a cup of water. Uncle Rufus opened up a can of beer and poured it into a glass cup.

"Dammit I'm outta cigarettes. Go to the store and get me a pack of Cools since y'all asses ain't in school. Make yo self-useful. Even if you was in school, ya Black asses ain't learnin shit up there fightin!"

Me, JD, and Casey left the house and headed to the liquor store.

"Man, you talk too damn much!" I told JD

Casey started laughing, "That nigga more scared of Mama than he is the police."

We cracked up laughing.

Chapter 27

Fatta Man

On our way back from the store we spotted Fatta Man standing on his front porch. He waved us over. Fatta man was 5'5 fat around the waist. We would steal cartons of cigarettes and liquor for him and he would throw us out a few dollars.

Standing on his porch he said in his raspy voice, "Gotta job. Pays $500 bones. Let me know." He focused on Casey. "If your brother want it." He was talking about Kory.

Casey said, "If we down he down."

Then Fatta man looked at me and JD and said, "Alright! It's a black 1989 Caddy, 4050 St. Louis Avenue. Take it to the ill Side. Come see me when you put it in the oven." Then he turned around and disappeared behind his screen door.

At the last minute, Fatta Man told Kory that the pickup point was changed. That same night, Kory went by Fatta Man's house to get the key for a pickup truck. We waited at the end of the block for Kory to pull up in the truck. We spotted an army green pickup driving down the block. Kory parked the truck and hopped out. "One of y'all gotta drive. Need to get my tools ready." He handed me and Casey a pistol smiling, "Fatta Man wanted us to have protection." He tucked his pistol in the back of his pants. Then he climbed into the cab of the truck.

Casey hopped in the passenger seat and I got behind the wheel. The new spot was a bar on Martin Luther King called the Diplomat. A bar where old heads like Aunt Irene and Uncle Rufus would hand out. When I spotted the Cadillac, I parked at a lot across the street from the bar and killed the headlights. The traffic was steady. Some of the old heads was leaving the club hopping in shiny new cars and some beat up rusted cars too. We sat and watch the scene until everybody was inside the bar. After a few minutes, Kory jumped out the cab and walked up to the Caddy. In one move, he had the driver's door opened.

He slid inside the car and the motor started humming. Kory droves away from the bar and I followed him down MLK then to Kings highway then to Highway 70 from there we drove across the MLK bridge to Illinois.

"Damn where this fool going? We been driving forever!" I said to Casey.

"You know he got all kinds of spots on the ill side, D." Casey said.

"He need to make it quick man. I don't like fuckin around over here on the ill side, man."

We exited the highway and Kory turned into an empty lot with tall grass and pitch-black dark. I kept the engine running.

Kory got out of the Cadillac and ran to the pickup truck and pulled his tool bag out the truck bed. A few minutes after he got back to the Caddy, a huge ball of fire and thick smoke rose up to the dark sky. Cory jumped ran back to the truck and hopped into the flatbed and I speed to the highway across the Poplar Street bridge back to St. Louis. Once we was back in the hood, I drove straight to Fatta Man's house, parked the pickup truck in his backyard. We all pulled out our guns wiped them down to get rid of prints and stuffed them under the front seat like we always did.

Cory knocked on Fatta Man's screen door and he appeared behind the screen with no noise like he was waiting for us. He asked in that scrapy voice, "Is that oven going?"

"That muthafuckah blazin!" Cory said handing Fatta Man the keys to the pickup. Fatta man took the keys disappeared behind the screen door for a minute then came back. He opened the door and handed Cory five one-hundred-dollar bills. Then he went back into the house and slammed his front door. Me, Cory, and Casey walked home staying away from the main streets, we walked down alleys and cut thru backyards. When we got to Aunt Irene's house, we hit the basement and Cory gave us our cut of the money.

Chapter 28

Gigi's Closet

"Danny! Wake up, my mom's is coming!"

I felt Gigi shaking me awake. I sat up in the bed wiping the sleep out my eyes.

She whispered, "Hide in my closet."

I jumped out the bed snatching up my clothes that was laying at the foot of her bed.

Gigi opened the closet door and I walked in. After she closed the door, I heard her mom's voice. I stood still. They talked for a moment then left. I hurried up and put my clothes on. Gigi's clothes that was hanging on the hangers hit me in the face. Dressed I sat down and listened to Gigi and her mom and Gigi walking in and out of her bedroom trying to act normal.

A memory flashed in my head of my Mama fussing at me and Lil Michael about dragging and moving slow in the morning. I missed the smell of my Mama's pancakes.

All of a sudden, the music on Gigi's boombox was turned up and then the closet door opened up, Gigi stuck her head in, "I don't know what to do?"

I whispered, "Just go to school and I'ma stay here until she leave."

"She won't leave till later." She whispered back. Then her mother started calling for her to come to the kitchen.

"Be right back." She whispered then shut the closet door.

A few minutes later the door opened and this time Gigi handed me a plate of food. The plate was loaded with a stack of three pancakes, scrambled eggs, sausage, and hashbrowns. She closed the closet door and the music on the boom box stopped. I took a bite of the pancakes and chewed slowly. With every bite of the food, memories of Mama, Lil Michael, and Derrick flooded my mind. Living with my Aunt Irene and five boys and one smart mouth girl was no joke. Aunt Irene was a good cook but she was no match for my mom's. I missed the smell of her kitchen and the peace of our house before she moved Larry in.

After I finished eating, I fell asleep until I heard Gigi's Mom on the telephone and walking around the house singing church songs.

I thought about the torch job and how we had to split the money three ways. Lil Michael needed some clothes and new shoes, the last time I saw him he was looking dusty. And Mama was still in the hospital. Then that nigga Nine popped in my head, now that's some real bread. Right then and there sitting in my girl's bedroom closet I made up my mind to find this hood nigga they call Nine. I will never forget the date, it was November 19, 1990.

Chapter 29

Roof Top

"Mr. Holmes, can I start you off with any drinks this afternoon."

Every Tuesday, I took Mama out to lunch at this five-star restaurant overlooking downtown St. Louis, the Roof Top. While we dined, we overlooked the entire city.

"Two glasses of your house wine." I ordered

"Yes, Sir coming right up." The waiter answered then disappeared.

"Has that man been back to the bakery?" Mama asked

"Nah I ain't spotted him."

The waiter came back, he placed the wine glasses in front of us. Both glasses was filled with golden champaign.

"Son when you gonna get a special lady in your life?"

I slid Mama a fat manilla envelope with ten thousand dollars stuffed in it. Mama smiled and slipped the envelope in her purse. Every Tuesday, I gave Mama an envelope stuffed with money. One week it would be $20,000 the next week $10,00 for the bills at her house, clothes and food for her, my sisters, and my daughter.

"I already have six women in my life Mama."

She smiled because she knew I was talking about her, my four sisters, Tanisha, Leah, Salena, Michelle, and my daughter Ayanna.

The waiter appeared at our table. "Can I take your orders?"

"Bring us the lobster and filet mignon." I told him.

Ten minutes later two waiters sat our plates down in front of us. Me and Mama was enjoying the smells coming from the gourmet food. I allowed Mama to enjoy her food for a few minutes before I dropped the bomb.

"Mama?"

Mama wiped her mouth with the cloth napkin.

"Yeah son."

"I saw Daddy a few weeks back." I avoided her eyes. I picked up my wine glass starring at the gold bubbles like they had answers.

"How is he?" she asked.

"The same."

"Where did you see him?"

"Downtown...he asked about you?"

Mama looked out the window like she was searching for a far-off memory of my dad and how he used to be.

"Still living on the streets hunh?" she asked her voice cold. Mama never forgave Daddy for leaving us. He told us he was going to work and never came home.

"Mama! I want to help him, get him off those streets."

"Hush that talk, Alex!"

"But that's my dad!"

"I know that's your Daddy but he past helping."

She held out her hand and I grabbed it. My hand swallowing up her small hand.

"You have done enough for this family. Baby when you gon settle down and get married?"

"Not now, I got too much going on." Then my cell phone ranged.

"Speak!"

"Man, one of the lookouts said the plain cars been rolling near the Furnace." It was Rasheed.

"Ain't no thing the Furnace is empty."

"Uhh..."

"What?" Anger was rising from my chest to my temples.

"Bae Bae had to cook the last of the ribs." Rasheed used code. Dope was still inside the house and Bae Bae was there cooking.

I stepped away from the table and into the restroom. "Nigga get Bae Bae outta there! I don't give a damn about shit in that house but Bae Bae!"

"On it Boss. We a block away."

"It's yo head if Bae Bae get caught up. Hit me on the line when yo ass done!" Then I slammed my phone shut.

Bae Bae turned out to be a real G in the kitchen cooking up dope just like Mac. It wasn't a day that went by that we wasn't together. Bae Bae was more than my chef, she was my nigga.

Chapter 30

St. Ferdinand Ave

After Gigi's Moms left the house, I took a shower, got dressed and snuck out the back door. I headed to the block of St. Ferdinand and Marcus Ave. It was around 11am and the block was waking up. Dope fiends walked down the street in a daze. I spotted some of Nine's foot soldiers. Two of em was sitting on the porch of a two-family flat and one sat in a black Cutlass.

"What up?" I spoke before I reached the porch steps.

"Sup." One of them said the other one was mean mugging me and I spotted him resting his hand on the Glock tucked in his waist. I knew them niggas was holding heat.

"I need to holla at Nine man." I got down to bidness.

"Yo my man, Nine bounced." The tall one said

"Who you?" the short light-skinned dude with his hand on his gun asked.

"Tell Nine Danny need to holla at him."

The tall one said, "Hold up! Ain't you Legend's Lil brotha?"

My stomach knotted up at the sound of my brother's street name. "Yeah!" I said real cool

"Damn what's up wit Legend how dat nigga doing?" the tall one asked then he turned to the short light skinned dude, "Yo that fool Legend, he a goon!"

Light skinned kept his eyes posted on me.

"When Nine gon be back on the block?" I asked the tall dude that knew my brother.

"Don't know."

"Awight then." I said and bounced.

Around ten o'clock that night I went back to the block. I wasn't gon wait to get put on. It was two soldiers posted on every corner. Cars was pulling up and driving off like a drive thru. The latest rap songs blasting from the car stereos. I got hype when I spotted some soldiers pulling up in candy painted rides, parking and running up to the dope house to drop off money. As I got closer to the steps of the dope house, I spotted Nine sitting on the porch steps five of his soldiers surrounding him. He was the same cat I saw in Skate King except he was looking more street this time. He was smoking on a cigarillo with a automatic rifle resting on his lap and a red and white Cardinals baseball cap cocked to the left side of his head.

I climb one step and a dark as midnight dude stepped up to me, "Fuck you want?"

I saw one of the soldiers lean over and say something to Nine.

"Blackboy kick back, he cool." Nine told him.

"Heard you Legend's Lil brotha?" Nine said.

"You heard right. I'm looking for work." I told him

He stood up still clutching his automatic rifle, "Follow me."

His soldiers mean mugged me but they moved out the way so I could walk up the steps.

Nine opened the door to one of the apartments. I followed him in. Inside the apartment looked like a factory. Work tables was lined up and on one side of the room dudes was stuffing dollar bills in a money machine and on the other tables soldiers was weighing and bagging dope. Nobody was talking or laughing it was straight business.

"You ready to make real dough?" Nine asked me.

"Hell yeah." I said.

"Let me kick it to you like this. I'ma bring you on but if some shit go down..."

"Don't trip I can handle mine." I told him.

"Be here tomorrow same time." Nine told me.

"I'm wit that." I said.

Chapter 31

Gimme That Heat

The next night before I had to report to the block, I went to see Gigi, kicked it with her then I caught up with my cousin Casey. Casey was outside with one of his homeboys. They was standing near that big tree that was in front of Aunt Irene's house smoking a blunt.

"Casey let me holla at you?"

Casey handed the blunt to his homeboy after he took a puff.

"I need to borrow the burner." I told him

Casey blows out the smoke not saying nothing.

"Come on man quit playin!" I said

"Nigga don't rush me. I'm tryin to figure out what's up wit you askin me for my burner."

"Don't trip I'ma get it back to you."

He started walking to the house. When we got inside of Aunt Irene's house, we headed straight to the basement door and then down the steps. He stopped at the bottom of the steps.

"Wait a minute hold up you got static wit some niggaz?" he asked me.

"Naw it ain't like that. I got this hustle going on and I ain't going into the jungle without some heat." I said.

He said nothing just went to grab the silver Glock.

"Is the clip full?" I asked him holding the Glock in my hand.

"Damn right, what you think I'ma sloppy nigga? Take care of my shit."

"I got you." I said and headed for the steps.

He yelled out, "Say, what's up with this hustle?"

"I'ma see what's up wit it then I'm bringing you, JD, and Cory in."

"What is it nigga?"

"I'll check you later Cuz."

Chapter 32

1st Night on Tha Block

As soon as I hit the block, I reported to Nine's dope house. Nine wasn't there but one of his Lieutenants gave me some stones and told me which corner to post up.

"Hold this." He handed me a 22 pistol. I tucked it in my back. Casey's silver Glock was tucked in my side waist. It was humid and hot outside but I was glad I wore a long Polo shirt and some jean shorts. My tennis shoes was old but I knew soon as I got my paper up, I could buy me and my Lil brother Michael some new kicks and fresh clothes.

It was so much action going on the heat didn't bother me. I checked out how the other corner boys was working, who was paying attention to the cars that drove by and the dope fiends that was on foot. It was a total of six of us on the corner two on each corner. It was this serious cat that rocked a wave cap and we shared a corner. He didn't say much just kept his head on a swivel. The niggas across the street from us was laughing and joking.

I reported to the same set every night at ten o'clock and worked the corner until the sun came up. After working my shift, I would sneak into Aunt Irene's basement door and fall asleep on one of the couches. I would wait until school ended then go check out Gigi and stay at her house until it was time to report back to the block. She would hold on to my paper for me. I didn't want to hide it at Aunt Irene's house, it was too many people going in and out like a Greyhound bus station.

Chapter 33

Heart

It was the first week in November, a little after 1am on a Friday night. The streets were slick from the rain that drenched the city all day and the ice in the wind was relentless. I watched the corner boys from the second floor of my apartment building that I had just purchased the month before. It was a four-family flat. One of the units was vacant and I kept it that way so that I could float in and out and watch my operation. The only person that knew about the new place was Bae Bae. I would slip in thru the back door. On this night Bae Bae was standing next to me watching everything. The street was bursting with life. Cars lined up like it was rush hour.

"This place is jumping!" Bae Bae said.

"It's always like this on the first of the month. Don't nobody sleep."

"St. Ferdinand is the money maker."

"Simple Ave is holding its own too."

"Take me to the Flame later I wanna get some ribs."

I spotted a four-door sky blue Cadillac cruising slow but the crazy thing was the passenger hung his head and torso out the window and aimed his gun at one of the corner boys and started spraying bullets everywhere. The corner boys scattered and customers speed off. The Cadillac tried to take off but the Legend's Lil brother fired back.

"Oh shit, Nine did you see that?" Bae Bae screamed

Lil dude threw his Glock on the pavement and reached down into his ankle and pulled out another gun and kept chasing the Caddy until it got away from him.

"Damn that Lil nigga got some heart!" I yelled out. "I need to go out there and check me some punk ass niggas." I snatched my mini-Uzis from the card table. Bae Bae followed me.

When I got reached the corner, I barked, "Did y'all see who them niggas was?" All the soldiers surrounded me.

"Naw I ain't never seen em before Nine." One of the corner boys spoke up.

"What the fuck y'all doing out here? Talking to bitches, laughing, and acting like hoes. My Lil nigga..." I pointed to Legend's Lil brother.

I asked him, "What's yo name again Lil dude?"

"Danny!" he told me.

I told him, "I'ma call you D'Hustle." Everybody started laughing.

"D'Hustle was holding it down while you bitch made niggas ducking and hidin."

Everybody was silent.

"Ya'll should've pumped some bullets in that Caddy." I barked.

"Yeah that mutha should've been looking like Swiss cheese." Rasheed said standing next to me. He must've came out of the dope house after he heard the gun shots.

"Damn right." I said

"Aye I think we need to shut it down for tonight in case they swing back and shoot up the set." Rasheed said.

"Awight bitches we gon shut it down and move everything in." I turned to Rasheed. "Have some of em stand post and give each nigga two straps."

"I'm on it." Rasheed turned to the corner boys giving orders.

Chapter 34

Deep in Them Streets

"I dig how you kept coming for them fools." Wave cap said giving me dap. "Nobody on the set got capped cause if they did the police will shut every muthafuckin thing down."

"No doubt." I said.

Me and Wave cap was posted in one of Nine's cars. I was sitting in the driver's seat and Wave cap sat on the passenger side. Nine had five Cutlasses in different colors, navy blue, black, burgundy, and champaign gold. The cars was for moving dope and money. When Nine popped up on the corner after the shoot out, I was shocked. I hadn't seen him in weeks. He was dressed in a Polo hoodie, a gold chain, a gold nugget watch, and some Timberlands that you won't find at the Flea Market. His whole outfit looked like it cost $1500. Seeing that shit made me want to grind even harder.

After Nine hopped in his Range Rover, Rasheed and Black Boy gave orders for some of the corner boys to sit in cars and other soldiers to surround the dope house. We was on the lookout for any strange cars that sped down Marcus Ave or St. Ferdinand. Customers had to come up to the door to buy product.

I was high on adrenaline that night. The gunplay had me pumped but I kept a blank face but on the inside I was like yeah "I love that gangsta shit! Show no fear D'Hustle."

For the rest of the night, we sat in silence watching customers come and go. Clocking every car that rolled by while keeping our fingers on the trigger.

When my shift was done on the block, I headed to Aunt Irene's. I slipped in the basement door from the backyard like I always did and

I passed out on the couch. An hour into my sleep, I felt somebody shaking me. I shot up and reached for my Glock but realized I was in my Auntie's basement and not on the block. Casey was standing in front of me.

"Wake up they looking for you upstairs." Casey said

"Who?" My heart was pounding in my chest. Then I heard my Mama's voice.

"Danny boy get up here!"

My eyes got big. I ran up the steps. Sitting at the kitchen table was my Mama and Aunt Irene. Mama had on a purple robe that had a zipper in the front. Her hair was pulled back into a ponytail. Since my Mama got out the hospital she slept in Aunt Irene's bedroom. Aunt Irene moved into her daughter, Candy Cane's room. I would check in on Mama every day and when I opened the bedroom door, Mama would be sleep barely moving.

I sat across from my Mama. Her skin was pale, her eyes was sunken in and her arms were bony. Mama reminded me of a skeleton. It took everything in me to hold back the tears. Ever since her no-good ass boyfriend Larry got killed by my brother, it seemed like Larry was sucking the life out of her from the grave.

"You ain't been going to school?" Her voice was brittle

I hung my head down cause I couldn't lie to my Mama.

"Danny boy don't lie to me!"

"No! I been working Mama."

"Where?" Aunt Irene barked she had to put her two cents in.

I had to think of a quick lie but Casey saved me.

"He working for them Arabs." Casey said leaning against the sink.

"Yeah, Mama I stock shelves for them. You know the store on Vandeventer."

"Danny boy you better get to that school or I'ma beat you. You hear me. You not ending up like your brother." Mama could barely stand on her own two feet. She never whipped me nor Lil Michael only Derrick.

I stood up and I kissed her forehead. "Yes Ma'am." Then I headed back down to the basement to get some sleep. Casey followed me.

"Aye I know you been over on that dope set working." He said

"Nigga how you know?"

"Chance told me."

"He talk like a bitch."

"Where my gun at?"

I reached under the couch and pulled it out.

"Keep it. You gon need it. But for real though Danny, St. Ferdinand is a shady set. Fatta Man got some work lined up for us."

"Man that ain't no bread." I told him.

I reached in my pocket and pulled out my wad of cash and held it up. "St. Ferdinand getting me that dough." Then I peeled off $200 and handed it to him. "For the gun."

He took it shaking his head. "You a hard head ass nigga."

Chapter 35

Steppin Up in Tha Game

"I wanna bring that lil dude on."

It was me, Rasheed, and Black Boy sitting in the Chinese restaurant on Tucker Ave in downtown St. Louis. It was the spot to get the real Chinese food. Every time I stepped foot in the door, the smell of fried rice, onions, and noodles would be calling me and my crew. That day our table was packed with plates of special fried rice, egg rolls, St. Paul sand whiches, and cans of Vess sodas. This was our spot because I knew the owners. They knew what we like to eat.

We didn't have to go to the counter and order. We would find a table and they would bring out the food. Before I came up in the streets I worked there, after my Daddy left us. The owners, Mr. Lee and his wife was the only people that gave me a job. I peeled shrimp, washed dishes, took out the trash, cleaned and swept the dining area. I had to do what I had to do to help my Mama.

"Who dat?" Black Boy frowned.

"What's the Lil dude's name that shot at the Caddy the other night, Legend's Lil bro."

"Danny!" Rasheed reminded me.

"Yeah, I named him D'Hustle." I remembered out loud.

There were customers standing at the counter ordering food and one homeless man sitting in the dining room.

"He already on." Rasheed said.

"Naw he mean give him some rank." Black Boy said then he bit into an egg roll.

"Where you gon put him Nine? He too young to run the stash houses, what you gon have him do? Drive you around?" Rasheed asked in between forkfuls of fried rice.

"I think you moving out too soon on em." Black Boy said.

I ate the last piece of my chicken St. Paul sand which, gulped down my grape soda, wiped my mouth and said, "He gon do pickups and drop offs."

Rasheed and Black Boy was quiet.

"You think he ready?" Rasheed spoke up

"Black Boy, I want you to school him." I said then the homeless guy walked over and stood next to our table.

He focused on Black Boy, "Say brother can you spare a dollar?"

Rasheed got angry, "Get the fuck away from here man, naw we ain't got shit." The man darted away from our table.

I reached in my pocket and pull out a wad of bills. I peeled off five twenty-dollar bills. I handed the money to Black Boy. "Give this to him."

Black Boy caught up with him "Aye!" Black Boy yelled. The man turned around and Black Boy shoved the bills into the man's dirty hand.

"Damn Nine you can't be giving these muthafuckahs money man. Shit you the Welfare office now?" Rasheed joked.

"Man, gon wit that shit. Let's roll." I fired back. Every time I saw a homeless man, I thought about my dad.

My Dad fought in the Vietnam War. He was a soldier in the U.S. Army. When he returned from Vietnam, he was a new man, quiet, withdrawn not the loving family man and best friend he was to me before he went overseas. My Dad loved music and he loved to laugh. Taught me to play chess and checkers. But after the war he shut himself off from the world and found peace and comfort in Vodka, beer, whiskey anything that numbed the memories of war.

Chapter 36

The Life

"Beep, Beep, Beep!" My pager went off.

I was at my girl Gigi's house. Her Mom was at work and her dad was on the road. We was laid up in her bed. I jumped out the bed to check my pager. It was on her pink and purple desk.

It was the block. I had to go to work. "Baby I have to go!"

"Why?" she sounded angry

"Gigi, I ain't going there wit you!"

She sat up in the bed. "When you coming back to school?"

"Soon!" I said and started putting on my underwear.

"I'm getting tired of this, you don't come to school anymore, what's up with you Danny?"

"You know what's up girl. I'm out there tryin to make some moves."

"What the hell does that mean?" she asked

I ignored her and kept putting my clothes.

"Danny!"

"Yeah Gigi."

"I know you work for Nine."

I didn't say shit.

"Are you gon answer me?"

"Quit trippin damn." I said

"What? You the one trippin." She said putting her bra and t-shirt on.

"Look Gig, I told you, later for that shit. I gotta go."

Dressed in her t-shirt and panties she led the way to the kitchen back door. I grabbed her by the waist. "Baby I'ma see you tomorrow."

She pushed me away. "Don't worry about ever coming over."

I froze, "What?"

She turned her back to me, "You heard me, Danny."

"I'ma, forget you said that shit. Like I said I'll see yo ass tomorrow." And I left.

I walked and jogged down the alleys dogs barking and jumping on fences. I had to push

Gigi out my mind until I finished business on the block. She kept sweating me about school. School wasn't shit because in one month I made five thousand selling stones on the corner.

When I made it to the spot, Black Boy said, "D'Hustle my man." He gave me five. I ran up the six steps to where Nine was sitting with Rasheed. Nine had his Desert Eagle 9 mm resting on his lap.

Nine yelled, "Black Boy, let's do this."

Shit I was getting nervous. I kept quiet but I kept my head on a swivel. If shit got thick, I had my Glock ready.

Nine went inside one of the apartments first. It was a four-family flat. I thought he was gonna go to the stash apartment where all the soldiers report to but he opened up the apartment front door on the right. I was thinking which of them I was gonna kill first.

Nine went into the apartment first, then Rasheed, then I did, then Black Boy. We all sat in the living room. The couches was tight. This apartment looked lived in not like the stash house.

I chilled when Nine sat the Desert Eagle 9mm on the glass end table.

"D'Hustle, you done on the corner." Nine started off. I was confused but I showed no fear.

"You gon be making drop offs and pickups with Black Boy. And once you got that shit down Black Boy gon leave you be." Nine explained.

I was fucked up but I didn't show it.

"Awight let's hit it, the first pick up is in a hour." Black Boy said checking the time on his pager.

Chapter 37

Slippin

"You Black Boy! You want me to take that nigga out? Northside asked
It was Northside, Black Boy, and Dirty Red. Black Boy called them and
gave the order to meet him at the White Castle lot on Kings highway and
Natural Bridge.
"Naw, nigga, just do like I told you." Black Boy said.
"Gotch you!" Northside said and stuffed a mini castle burger in his mouth.
"Black my man after we fuck him up real good and we rob his punk ass,
we keepin the loot?"
"If you keep that shit that's y'alls muthafuckin payment." Black Boy said.
"How much we talkin, Black?" Dirty Red asked
"Enough bread for y'all niggas to bounce back."

Chapter 38

Caught Slippin

"Speak." I answered my cell phone while making a left turn on Goodfellow Ave.

"Danny where you at?" It was my cousin Casey on the other end.

"Black Boy got me droppin off some groceries (that was code talk for dropping off dope) on the West side."

"Shit man that's a bad set. Why you didn't ask me or JD to go wit you?"

"It's all good. I'ma get back at you in a minute. I just pulled up."

We hung up.

The address that Black Boy gave me was a four-family flat but you had to go inside a hallway to get to the apartments. The sun had gone down but I could still see the address. Nobody was out on the block, it was quiet.

I popped the trunk to my Regal and took out the grocery bags that was packed with Pringle potato chip cans and packs of Chips Ahoy cookies. Coke was packed inside of the Pringle cans and weed was packed inside the cookie packs.

I scanned the block before the closed the trunk and walked away from the car. I did a mental check, "My Glock tucked in my waist and a .45 on my ankle.

I opened the main door to the apartments. The hallway was dim except for a small dim light shining by the mailboxes in the wall. I climbed two steps, on the third step I heard something and turned around then I felt steel hit my nose and blood squirted out. I dropped the grocery bags to reach for my Glock but then somebody came from behind me and him me in the back of my head. I fell down the steps. When I hit the floor, four pair of legs started kicking me in my head and ribs.

"Get tha dope." I heard one of em yell to the other ones.

Then another one said, "Check that niggas's pockets." I felt one of them reach inside my pants pockets and snatch out my three thousand dollars.

I tried to sit up but one of them hit me across the face with a gun I fell to the floor then I balled as they kept kicking me. I was able to grab my .45 from my ankle. I pulled the trigger and it sounded like fire crackers going off.'

"'Shit, I been hit." One of them said.

I kept shooting and they all ran out the building.

I was able to get to the Regal and start the ignition and drive off. As I sped down Martin Luther King Blvd my head felt like missiles was exploding inside. When I stopped at the red light at MLK and Kings highway, my vision got funny. The headlights from the other cars blended together and my head felt like I was underwater. When the light turned green, I sped off determined to get to my Aunt Irene's house. I made it to Aunt Irene's house and then everything went dark.

To Be Continued...

About the Author

Dakota Wright has experience in story telling. Prior to becoming a fiction author, she was Chief Editor of a music magazine, Pass Da Mic. Currently she lives on the West Coast where she is raising her daughter and writing captivating flash fiction. Please feel free to email Dakota at Backstory314@gmail.com with any questions or comments.

About the Publisher

Silver Maple Publishing offers publishing opportunities for up and coming authors. We look for fiction, poetry, and memoirs.

Please visit our website at www.silvermaplepublishing.com